For the Sake of a Child

By

Stevie Turner

For the Sake of a Child

Dedication

Dedicated to my friend Sandra, taken from us too soon.

Synopsis

Ginny Ford is pleased to win the coveted job of housekeeper to the directors of PhizzFace Inc. However, her joy becomes tarnished by an accidental find whilst cleaning, leading her to suspect that all is not as it should be on the managerial corridor. Delving deeper, she is shocked to uncover a secret paedophile network that has remained hidden for years, involving the very people she has come to know and trust. Unable to live with her conscience, she decides that she cannot keep quiet and that she must find a way of helping all the children involved. However, by speaking out against her employers, Ginny realises too late that she has put her entire family in danger.

Table of Contents

PART 1
CHAPTER 1

NERVOUSLY SMOOTHING DOWN her regulation blue PhizzFace overall with one hand and clutching her coat and bag with the other, Ginny Ford took a deep breath, checked for stray strands of dark hair that might have escaped from her bushy ponytail, and knocked on the office door.

"Come in."

"Hi Bob. You wanted to see me?" Ginny forced a grin and decided not to let on how terrified she felt.

"I expect you're wondering what this is all about." Bob Fenton waved an arm in the direction of an empty chair.

Ginny nodded and sat down carefully on the edge of the seat, arms and legs crossed, in a psychological effort to ward off any barbed words that might be cloaked in her supervisor's usual banal banter.

"Emma's decided not to come back after her annual leave. The Misters tell me they're more than pleased with the job you've been doing in the factory; you're reliable and one of our longest serving housekeepers. If you want the directors' corridor, then the job's yours. There'll be the usual pay rise for the top floor, as you know, and you'll be able to earn more for the extra hours spent clearing up after the conferences."

Ginny wondered if she had heard him right. For a moment she was too shell-shocked to speak.

"Emma's left? But why would she want to leave?" Ginny thought of her friend struggling to bring up her boys alone. "She's got two kids depending on her."

"She's obviously found something better, so good luck to her. What do you say? Do you want the job or not?"

Ginny felt an unusual impatience in Bob's voice. Relaxing back into her seat, she shot him one of her full-on smiles.

"Of course I do! What do you take me for? Who wouldn't want the top corridor?" She felt a growing happiness at the thought of it.

"That's settled then. I'll let Mister Randolph know. You'll be handing your job over to Sue tomorrow, so start on Monday morning, six o'clock sharp as usual. There'll be some extra hours in the kitchen on quite a few Mondays after you drop Trudi off at school due to the Misters sometimes having Friday afternoon conferences, so just fill in this timesheet and I'll make sure you get paid for them." He handed over a piece of A4 paper.

"Great. Thanks Bob." She took the single page from him and gazed briefly at the unfamiliar timesheet before popping it into her bag. "I hope I can get my head around this."

"You'll be fine. There's a brain inside that curly head of yours. See you tomorrow.

The polished granite and marble foyer of PhizzFace Incorporated was just beginning to buzz with early-morning activity as Ginny made her way up the stairs from her supervisor's office in the basement to the ground floor. The decorative fountain in the middle of the foyer was trickling, and the sound of water bouncing off the smooth pebbles around the base always made her want to pee. She hated going out through the revolving doors, and as usual opened the disabled entrance door which was slightly off to the right.

"See you in the morning, Ginny."

"'Bye, Will." She waved to the smiling concierge as she passed him by.

The extra ten minutes spent with Bob had made her late; she knew Larry would be champing at the bit to get to the office. At the zebra crossing she willed the traffic to stop; hopping impatiently from foot to foot. By the time she had run down Frobisher Street and zoomed left into Grove Gardens she could see her husband and daughter waiting; both were looking expectantly in her direction. One of the pair was wearing a thunderous expression, and the other one was swinging rather nonchalantly on the garden gate.

"Where have you been? I've got to go!"

"Sorry, but I've got some good news to tell you later on." She gave him a quick peck on the cheek as he ran past her towards the car. "Come on Missy, school time." She took her daughter's hand and exhaled a loud sigh of joy, coupled with some relief.

"What good news, Mummy?"

Seven year old Trudi was as sharp as a tack; arty and creative just like herself. Ginny smiled fondly at her daughter as she squeezed her fingers.

"Mummy's got a pay rise and the cushiest job of all." She glanced down at her daughter to make sure she was holding a lunch box in her other hand, as they began the short walk to school.

"Doing what?"

"Cleaning the offices of the five PhizzFace directors."

"Why is it good?"

"Because they don't make a lot of mess."

"Why can't you just stay at home and write more books?"

"I told you; because I can't find an agent to sell them for me, and I need to earn some money but still look after you while I'm doing it."

"Why can't you sell them yourself then?"

"I try to, but not many people want to buy them."

"Why not?"

"Because there's thousands and millions of other writers out there all trying to sell *their* books at the same time."

"Why can't you sell them at a different time then?"

Her daughter's constant questions began to grate on her nerves. Ginny steered Trudi around the end of Grove Gardens and into Arcadia Road.

"I can see Tom Osborne! He's my boyfriend now!"

Trudi unclasped her hand from her mother's and raced ahead, while Ginny slowed her pace, smiled at her daughter's retreating back, and relished the sudden peace and quiet. At the entrance to the playground she waited slightly apart from the other chattering parents letting Bob's news sink in a bit further until the bell for lessons rang, returning the farewell wave from her daughter with a wave of her own. When the playground was empty Ginny quickly retraced her steps, looking forward to getting home to a cup of strong coffee and a hot shower.

After a refreshing wash she took advantage of the empty house and settled down in front of the computer to do some writing and networking, only rising when her stomach told her it was lunchtime. After a quick sandwich she worked through on a troublesome chapter until 2:45, when glancing at her watch, she reluctantly pulled her mind from her cyber world and walked briskly to the school playground. She again stood apart from the other mothers while searching briefly for her best friend Emma, but came to the conclusion that one or both of her children must be off sick.

"Has Robert been to school today?" Ginny kissed her daughter as she ran up to her in the playground.

"No; I haven't seen him." Trudi handed over her empty lunchbox and reading folder and skipped alongside her mother.

"He must have the chickenpox bug." Ginny smiled at Trudi. "Thank goodness you've already had it."

"Ryan's not at school either." Trudi waved to a classmate walking off in the opposite direction.

"He's probably got it as well."

Ginny always hated the first half an hour after Trudi had come home from school. There would always be the usual sighs and reluctance to read and complete homework, with Ginny always wanting to get the workbook signed and get it over with before her daughter became too tired.

"Any homework tonight?" Ginny crossed her fingers.

"Just reading." Trudi sighed.

"Let's do a couple of chapters, and then I can sign your homework book. Soon after that Daddy will be home and we'll be able to have dinner."

"What's for dinner? I can't smell anything cooking." Trudi wrinkled her nose.

"We'll see what's in the cupboard." Ginny stayed tactfully silent on the subject.

By the time she had overseen the reading and signed in the book, Trudi was complaining of being hungrier than the whole world. Ginny switched on the oven and took a large tray covered in silver foil from the fridge.

"What's in there?" Trudi began to lift up one corner.

"Fingers out; go and change your clothes, and dinner won't be long."

When she heard Larry's key turning in the lock, the table was set, the lasagne was bubbling, colourful vegetables were *al dente* in the steamer, and the wine was cooling in the fridge. Ginny kissed her husband and enjoyed the brief sensation of feeling safe with his arms around her.

"I never got to hear your good news this morning."

"I'll tell you over dinner. Just let me dish up first.

"Where's Trude?"

"In her room; give her a shout and tell her dinner's ready."

Ginny switched off the oven and steamer, and took three plates out from the warming tray under the grill.

"Bob's given me the directors' corridor, *and* I can earn more when there's been a conference." Ginny ladled lasagne and vegetables onto the plates.

"Trudi doesn't like lasagne." Larry returned to the kitchen and eyed the plates. "It's going to be another set-to to get her to eat anything."

"Are you listening?"

"Yeah; something about directors. What did you say?"

"Come and sit down and I'll tell you again."

Larry finished the last of his lasagne and put down his knife and fork.

"Good news about the job, but what if you have to work later on a Monday or in the school holidays?" He looked at her questioningly.

"I'm going round to see Emma after dinner; she's always home after seven o'clock. I'm going to ask her if she'd mind taking Trudi to school for me, or having her for a while any time I need to work extra hours. I'll obviously phone you if I need to stay after half past eight on Monday mornings, and you'll have to drop Trudi round there on your way to work. Emma won't mind though; I've looked after her two often enough."

Ginny poured herself some more wine and prepared herself for the upcoming battle of wills as she looked at her daughter's stony expression.

"Come on Trudi, eat a little bit more for Mummy please."

"I don't like lasagne."

"I'll give you a bit to eat and then you can have some pudding." Ginny made a small pile of food with her fork on one side of her daughter's plate.

"I don't want the meat thing. I only like the pasta."

"Okay; just eat the pasta then." Ginny was happy if her skinny daughter ate anything at all. "Would you like some yoghurt afterwards?"

"I don't like yoghurt."

"What *do* you like then?" Larry sat back in his chair and sighed.

"Chocolate." Trudi smiled at her father.

"You can't eat any chocolate if you don't eat some dinner." Larry sipped his wine and sighed.

"Oh Daddy, pl-ee-a-se…..my foot hurts!" Trudi inspected her ankle and took off her shoe.

"What's your sore foot got to do with not eating your dinner?" Larry put his glass down slightly too forcibly on the table, causing Ginny to wince.

"It's too painful to eat!"

Ginny sighed as she watched her daughter going through the same tried and tested routine.

"I'm definitely going to book an appointment for you to see the doctor tomorrow. There's obviously something terribly wrong with your foot. Perhaps it needs amputating." Larry rolled his eyes to the heavens. "This is enough to drive me to drink."

"What's amp-i-tating?" Trudi inched a sliver of pasta into her mouth and grimaced.

"Chopping it off; that'll stop it hurting." Larry shot Trudi a mean glance.

With the sudden realisation that her father was reaching the end of his shorter-than-average fuse, Trudi relented and tucked into some pasta.

"It feels a bit better now."

"Thank Christ for that." Larry sighed.

Opening the front door after dinner, Ginny let herself out; pleased that she was managing to dodge yet another April shower. She hurried along Grove Gardens towards the Merchant Estate, pressing the button for the lift to take her up to the sixth floor of Emma's tower block. The lift was slow in coming; in fact it was obvious after five minutes of waiting that the lift was not going to arrive at all. Trudging up the steep flights of steps, Ginny wrinkled her nose at the overpowering stench of urine on the stairwell. Panting, she opened the landing fire door leading to the four flats on the sixth floor, but was surprised and dismayed to see a padlock on the outside of number 25. At the sight of the padlock she felt rather silly ringing the bell, but felt that she ought to do it just to make sure Emma really was gone.

"Hello!" Ginny bent down and shouted through the letterbox. "Emma!"

She could see into the passageway; it was empty of any floor covering and furniture. The kitchen at the end of the passageway was also vacant. All she could see was one of the children's toys lying forlornly on the floor outside the kitchen.

"It's no use shouting; Emma and the kids moved out a week ago."

Perplexed, Ginny stood up and turned around at the sound of a voice emanating from the flat next door. She recognised Emma's friend Rita, who also had a child in Trudi's class.

"Where's she gone? She never said anything to me!" Ginny wanted to cry at the unwelcome news that her best friend had seemingly disappeared without a trace.

"All she said was that she had the chance of a better life for her kids, and that she was going to take it." Rita shrugged her shoulders.

"Did she win the lottery or something?" Ginny stared back at Emma's front door, stunned and disbelieving.

"Don't know. Don't know anything really. Removal men came to take all her stuff away, and she got in the van with the kids and they drove off."

Still in a disbelieving trance-like state, Ginny trudged back down the stairs and walked slowly home. On the way back she tried to ring her friend's mobile phone, but a robotic voice answered at the other end to say that the number was no longer available.

"What'll I do? I can't ask Mum and Dad; they live too far away, and are too old now anyway. I still can't believe that Emma's disappeared off the face of the earth. She was my best friend at work." Ginny cuddled up to Larry's warm chest later that evening in bed, and tried to stem the tears forming at the back of her eyes.

Larry kissed the top of her head.

"I thought I was your best friend?" He chuckled as he held her close. "She must have won the lottery; that's all I can think of."

"She hardly ever had enough money to play the lottery. It just doesn't make sense."

She gave in to the tears that could not be stopped no matter how hard she tried.

"Don't worry; I'm able to stay longer at work to make up for getting in late if you have to stay on. We'll work it out.

Don't cry." He kissed her again and gave her a reassuring squeeze.

"Love you, Larry. Of course you're my best friend; it's just that Emma…"

"I know; she was your mate; someone you could have a moan about men with."

"Something like that." Ginny sniffed and sighed.

"Give us a kiss. I'd slave away in the office over a hot computer 'til midnight every day if it'd make you happy."

"Silly sod. I'd never see you." She gave a rueful laugh through her tears as she kissed him.

"That's better. Give us another one."

"Do you still love me?" She kissed him and closed her eyes.

"Don't ask such bloody stupid questions." He sat up, turned off the bedside lamp, drew her towards him in the darkness, and with his hands and his tongue made her sorrows momentarily slip away.

CHAPTER 2

GINNY STEPPED OUT of the lift at the 15th floor and turned right. The thick blue carpet embedded with the PhizzFace logo that lined the directors' corridor felt spongy under her feet, and slightly muted any clanking that the unfamiliar key ring made as it jangled in the pocket of her overall. At six o'clock on a Monday morning not even a pin was dropping as she made her way to the kitchen which she had been told was down one end of the passageway. Nearest the lift on the left-hand side she passed the solid teak door guarding the office of Mr Randolph Veck, Managing Director. Opposite this she noted an identical door bearing the name of Mr Dennis Veck, Director. Towards the end window on either side were offices belonging to Assistant Directors Mr Charles Standen and Mr John Ridley. She checked every gilt embossed handle as she passed, but all of the doors were locked.

Trying to locate the kitchen, she quickly backtracked past the lift to the other end of the corridor, noting the double doors of the conference room on her left, and another teak door opposite the conference room belonging to Miss

Evelina Veck, Director. Finally, next to Miss Veck's office and to the right of a large window on the end wall she eventually found the kitchen. Opposite the kitchen and next to the conference room she saw male and female toilets, but still with the same teak entry doors and gilt lettering. None of the doors yielded to her touch.

Ginny felt like an intruder as she took the new key ring out of her pocket and tried a selection of keys in each door until she had unlocked all the rooms along the corridor. She made a mental note to colour code and name the keys with some of Trudi's stickers. She noticed that each office held its own particular smell when the door was pushed open, but she definitely preferred Miss Veck's domain, with its overtones of pot pourri and perfume. She wedged open the heavy doors with chairs, thinking it would then be easier to trundle the vacuum cleaner in and out.

The kitchen and conference room were neat and tidy. Feeling slightly disappointed that she would not be paid for any extra hours that day, Ginny set to work. She tore a bin liner off a roll she found in the kitchen drawer, and went to and fro between the offices emptying all the bins into the black sack, leaving it next to the lift for collection by the concierge as she had been instructed to do. She then unlocked the housekeeper's cupboard, finding in place a long cobweb brush, a bagless vacuum cleaner, and a mop and bucket, some bleach and various cleaning fluids. Next to spare rolls of lavatory paper stood a broom, a dustpan and brush, and a few cans of spray polish along with several square yellow dusters and pairs of brightly coloured rubber gloves.

Her orderly mind quickly formulated a plan; first the cobweb brush would be applied to all the ceilings. Then the kitchen sink and worktops could be wiped down and the kitchen tiles mopped. After this she would clean the toilets and sinks, polish the mirrors, and mop the lavatory floors. The conference table and the directors' office furniture could then be dusted and polished, and lastly she would run over all the carpets with the upright vacuum cleaner. If there had been a Friday afternoon conference she decided to clear any detritus from the conference table and then polish and vacuum, but do any washing up and cleaning of the kitchen last, possibly after the school run if Larry had to leave early. In this way she could shut herself in the kitchen and not be in the way when the offices were occupied after nine o'clock.

Feeling rather pleased with her plan she took out the cobweb brush and inspected the low false ceiling along the corridor, and identical ones inside the offices. There were quite a few fine silk webs dotted here and there, but none that the brush with its long extension could not reach.

The kitchen looked as if it had been recently cleaned. She opened the cupboards to find cups, dinner plates and side plates in regulation PhizzFace blue. There were also crystal glasses, decanters, teabags and coffee. A locked larder yielded to the smallest key, and revealed a large store of various bottles of wine, sherry, beer, whisky and gin. A fridge-freezer in the larder was well stocked with milk, pizzas, loaves of bread, oven chips, and a tub of ice cream. Ginny frowned in puzzlement. She could not imagine the imperious Mr Randolph ever picking up a slice of pizza with his well-manicured fingers; in fact she could not see him in her mind's eye enjoying pizza in any form at all, or giving it to his clients at a conference. On the few occasions she had seen him in the distance, he had seemed far too grand to ever consume anything less than the finest Beluga caviar off gold-rimmed square plates.

She wiped around the kitchen sink, and passed a cloth over the worktops. The floor was clean; likewise the lavatory floor, toilets and sinks. She checked the cubicles had enough lavatory paper, and then she polished the long mirror above the sinks and quickly mopped the floors.

Then it was time to start on the offices; the nearest one to her was that of Miss Evelina Veck. A large canvas photo taken many years before showed Evelina with her parents and brothers, and hung on the wall behind her desk. Looking at the photo and remembering her few glimpses of Mr Randolph, Ginny could see that in his youth PhizzFace's managing director had been extremely good looking, with darkish eyes and cherubic blond curly hair framing a square-jawed and sensitive looking face. Mr Dennis, shorter, slightly darker and more ordinary-looking in the photo, stared rather sulkily out into the distance, not quite looking at the camera. Evelina, obviously older than her brothers, stood smiling next to her mother, with one hand dropping down onto Dennis' shoulder.

Another photo Ginny picked up to dust showed Evelina presumably as she was now. Ginny had only glimpsed her briefly in passing a few times, but she was impressed at the older woman's flawless skin. She was very interested to find out if any of PhizzFace's products had caused such a halt in the march of time, or whether Evelina had possibly succumbed to the surgeon's knife on several occasions. She polished Evelina's large mahogany desk until it shone, and then carefully replaced each framed family photo back in its exact original spot. After vacuuming and dusting the rest of the furniture and watering the multitude of trailing plants, Ginny locked the office and moved further along the corridor.

The two Veck brothers' offices were almost completely identical, apart from Randolph's ticking clock on the wall and Dennis' digital clock on his desk. Ginny noticed that each office had a small ante-room for a secretary, with both rooms almost barren of furniture and personal possessions except for those which were absolutely necessary. She could see no family photographs on either desk; there were no pot plants, the shelves were empty, the leather Chesterfield sofas were unsullied, and the rooms seemed rather impersonal and unlived-in.

After cleaning through and locking the offices, she moved on to the last two on the corridor. She looked around; books and papers were stacked haphazardly on the shelves, there were dusty plants in corners, and spare coats and umbrellas draped over chairs. She was pleased to see that Mr Charles in particular looked like a happy family man, positively beaming out from the photograph on his desk, surrounded by his radiant wife and five adult children. Mr John she could see looked somewhat bemused, standing stiffly next to his wife in what was obviously a wedding photo. She looked around for photographs of Mr John's children, but there were none as far as she could see.

By the time she had cleaned all the offices and locked up, the time had moved on towards 08:15, but there would still be plenty of time to take Trudi to school. As she waited by the lift she noticed that Will had already noiselessly collected her bag of rubbish. She waved to him as she opened the door of the disabled entrance, and flashed him a smile when the concierge raised his arm in acknowledgment. Within ten minutes she was home.

"How did your first day go?" Larry picked up his car keys and gave his wife and daughter a kiss.

"No problem really. If you saw two of the offices you would think that nobody worked in there at all."

"Perhaps they're on the golf course all day."

"Lucky old them."

"Yeah."

CHAPTER 3

IT WAS NOT until the following week that Ginny was able to mark up her timesheet with some extra hours. When she unlocked the door to the conference room on the second Monday her heart sank slightly. Dirty plates, cutlery and cups littered the table; the carpet was covered in food crumbs, and the whole room looked as though a bomb had fallen upon it overnight.

Sighing, she piled the used crockery and cutlery onto a hostess trolley standing idle against a far wall. She wheeled the trolley, rattling and clanking, into the kitchen, saving the washing up and tidying of the kitchen until after she had cleaned the rest of the rooms along the corridor. She went over to her coat hanging up in the kitchen and took out her mobile phone, sending a text to Larry to let him know she would be late.

She began her cleaning routine as usual with the toilets, after the mandatory check for cobwebs. The women's cubicles and sinks seemed quite untouched from the week before, but she realised that cleaning the men's lavatories would take her rather longer than previously. Each toilet bowl needed a rigorous application of elbow grease, and every sink was grimy and stained.

Wrinkling her nose, she put on some rubber gloves, unscrewed the top of a bottle of bleach, and set to work. When at last she started on the final job of cleaning the kitchen, the time had moved on towards nine o'clock and Ginny could hear activity and voices in the corridor outside as she dried the last of the plates and put them away. As she sprayed disinfectant over the worktops, the door to the kitchen opened and a good-looking middle-aged man about six feet tall with silvery coloured hair just touching his collar stood framed in the doorway.

"Ah; you must be Ginny, our new housekeeper?"

"Hello." Ginny suddenly felt unusually shy.

"Allow me to introduce myself. I'm Randolph Veck." He held out his right hand. "I'm sorry for the mess today. It's not usually this bad." He smiled and looked down at her out of two twinkling hazel eyes.

"That's okay!" Ginny shook his hand and wished she was somewhere else. "I'm Ginny Ford."

"My brother Dennis and I would like you to have this." He handed over a crisp twenty pound note. "A little token of our appreciation for all your hard work this morning."

Ginny was taken aback at the director's generosity.

"Oh no! Really, that's not necessary!" She shook her head.

"I insist. Please, it would make us feel better!" He smiled and placed the note on the kitchen worktop.

"Well, thank you very much. I've almost finished now; I'll be out of your way in ten minutes." She picked up the money and put it in the pocket of her overall.

"Absolutely no rush. Come and meet Dennis. Nobody else is about just yet. "

Preferring to be gone, but not wanting to seem ungrateful, Ginny followed Randolph Veck down the corridor and stood awkwardly with him outside his brother's office as he lightly tapped on the door and opened it.

"Dennis; I'm just introducing Ginny to you, our new housekeeper" Randolph stood to one side as a man seemingly in his early fifties and about two inches shorter than his brother, well-built, and with slate grey hair got up from his chair.

"Come in my dear, come in!"

"Good morning, Mr Veck. Thank you for the twenty pounds." Ginny stepped into the office, but was uncharacteristically tongue-tied and wished the earth could swallow her up whole.

"Call me Dennis. No problem; I'm sorry we left the place in such a bad state."

"I think everywhere is shipshape now. Is there a conference every Friday?" As she struggled to think of something else to say, she looked at the two brothers and noticed a quick glance shoot between them.

"Probably every other Friday I'd say; it depends on what we need to discuss with our shareholders." Randolph Veck's reply was instant and glib.

"Well, thanks again for the money. I'll leave you in peace now and be on my way." She turned towards the door and freedom.

"Of course; goodbye Ginny."

"Goodbye, and thank you once again."

Later on that evening, Ginny sat next to Larry on a bench in the swing park and watched as their daughter waved to them from the top of a climbing frame.

"I met the Veck brothers this morning; they gave me a twenty pound tip for cleaning up all the extra mess." Ginny waved back. "Careful Trudi!"

"Perhaps they should have conferences more often." Larry chuckled.

"I can't believe Emma gave the job up. It just doesn't make sense to me."

"Well, just be grateful that they asked you to carry on with it. What time did you get home after all?"

"I was about an hour late. Thanks for taking Trudi to school. Did they mind at work?"

"Nah. That's the good thing about working for a newspaper; it's not a strictly nine to five business."

"Mummy! I'm stuck! I can't get down!" Trudi's wail alerted Ginny, who stood up.

"It's okay; I'll go up and get her. We'd better get her to bed after this anyway. It's getting late" Larry looked at his watch as he rose to his feet.

Ginny smiled at the sight of her agile and muscular husband shinning up the climbing frame to rescue his miniature damsel in distress. Although he possessed only a short fuse, his kindness knew no bounds, and taking her family, her writing, and her new cleaning job into consideration, all in all she thought herself a very lucky lady indeed.

CHAPTER 4

SPRING TURNED INTO early summer; her new teen romance novel was almost finished, and she had knocked at least ten minutes off her cleaning routine. One Tuesday morning in the middle of May Ginny plugged in her headphones, switched on her iPod, waved her feather duster around in the air like a lasso, and sang along loudly to a melody. She threw open the first office door she came to, and blushing, stopped dead in her tracks at the sight of a well-preserved lady of uncertain age, who was smiling at her from behind a computer screen.

"Sorry! I didn't think anyone would be about at six fifteen in the morning!" She turned off her iPod and pulled out the headphones, quickly putting them back in the pocket of her overall.

"Good morning; you must be Ginny. I'm Evelina Veck; sometimes I can't sleep so I come in early and get some work done. It's much more productive than lying awake doing nothing." Evelina stood up and held out her right hand.

"Hello." Ginny shook the proffered bejewelled hand trimmed with long fingernails painted a delicate blue, and wondered how anybody could look so good first thing in the morning.

"I'm only hearing good things about you. My office has never looked so clean and tidy."

"Thanks. Do you want me to clean in here today?" Ginny hoped fervently for a negative response.

"Yes that's fine. I like having someone to chat to, and you look like an intelligent girl. What do you do when you're not cleaning, my dear?"

"I'm a struggling writer; really struggling!" She chuckled.

"My goodness! You must bring one of your books in for me to read."

"They're mostly children's books, although I'm now working on a teen romance." She shifted awkwardly from one foot to the other.

"A teen romance? Aren't they all married and pregnant now at sixteen? Is there any romance left?" Evelina's grey eyes twinkled.

"I hope so. Well, I know I wouldn't like my daughter to be pregnant at sixteen."

Ginny was aware that Evelina's grey eyes were looking her up and down, and felt awkward and ill-at-ease as she carefully dusted and polished. She sensed the older woman's gaze boring into her back as she moved precious ornaments, and hoped against hope she did not drop anything out of nervousness.

"Tell me about your daughter. Have you any other children, my dear?" Evelina stopped typing and looked towards Ginny.

"One daughter, but no other children. Trudi's seven now and at Manorflower school, but seems to be going on seventeen. I have a picture of her in my locket here." She undid a heart-shaped necklace and displayed a prized photo.

"Oh! She's beautiful! She has your dark curly hair. They all grow up too soon these days don't they? I never married, and sadly neither did my brothers." Evelina smiled wistfully.

"I expect you were all too busy running the company." Ginny wished the woman would stop talking and let her get on.

"Absolutely. There's been no time for anything else. Did you know that there's not one heir between us? The whole organisation will pass to our only cousin Rupert when the last one of us dies."

Evelina's visage appeared momentarily melancholic. Ginny felt embarrassed, closed her locket, and edged towards the door.

"It's never too late. My mum was forty two when she had me."

"My dear, how old do you think I am?" Evelina smiled again; her sudden sadness apparently forgotten.

"Er………about forty five?" Ginny lied and took twenty years off the woman's age to make her feel better.

"I'm seventy eight. Randolph is seventy one, and Dennis is sixty nine. Our chances at procreation have long gone."

"Wow! I would never have thought any of you were the ages you are!" Ginny's jaw dropped, owing to the fact that she was truly and utterly amazed.

"It's why this company is so successful. Many years' ago our father Aldous was a successful doctor and pharmacist. He had the original idea of inventing an anti-ageing cream using water and an emulsifying agent combined with an apple-like fragrance and a preservative, which needed some work to make it right. Father was the company's first director, before succumbing to illness and handing it over to Randolph, Dennis and I. In his youth Randolph was also a pharmacist, and slaved away for years in the laboratory perfecting the PhizzFace 100 night cream. It took him one hundred revisions of the formula, hence the name, and eighteen years until he was satisfied with it. I've been using it since it was PhizzFace 12. It was obviously good enough then."

"It's amazing! The formula must be a very well-kept secret!" Ginny laughed as she tried unsuccessfully to spot any tell-tale tracks of the surgeon's knife on Evelina's face.

"It's in Randolph's head, but the rest of us have access to a safe deposit box if we ever need to refresh our memories. John and Charles of course have to know as they're more involved down on the factory floor with Randolph. Dennis and I are more in the marketing area."

"Now I know what to ask my husband to buy me for my birthday."

"Have you never used it?" Evelina's face registered complete surprise.

"Well…no, actually. It's a bit out of my price range unfortunately."

"Then you must have a jar now."

Evelina unlocked a drawer under her desk and fished around inside with her painted fingernails before bringing out a box. On seeing the contents unwrapped, Ginny recognised the large expensive cobalt blue glass jar moulded into the shape of an apple that she had seen advertised on TV, and which she knew was mainly sold in the most expensive London stores. Turning it around and checking that the product had not previously been opened, Evelina held out the jar.

"Here you are my dear; this should last you a good three months."

"I don't know what to say. It's so generous of you to give me this!" Ginny knew the cream in its pretty decorative container was worth at least eighty five pounds; probably more as it was of the larger size.

"I hope you never look a day older than you do now. How old *are* you, by the way?"

"Thirty four." Ginny, transfixed by the product in her hand, answered Evelina's questions on autopilot.

"You are a beautiful young woman with your life in front of you. Now you have the secret to eternal youth in your hands." Evelina laughed and resumed typing.

"Thank you so much." Ginny looked at her watch. "I must get on with the other offices now though. I'll bring in the vacuum cleaner later on."

"No, leave my room for today please. I have to make some phone calls, but do carry on with the other offices"

Ginny closed Evelina's door behind her and stepped out into the corridor carrying the heavy jar of night cream. She could not believe she had just been speaking to somebody who was nearly eighty years of age.

"My old Mum is seventy six, but Evelina looks young enough to be her daughter and she's two years' older." Ginny talked over her shoulder to Larry as she stood at the stove and mixed around a stir fry. "It's a bit eerie. She doesn't seem to be ageing at all."

"She can afford to have expensive surgery, love."

"I can't see where she's been under the knife. You can spot the old celebrities on TV who have had a face-lift; their skin's all tight and pulled up above their ears."

"Yeah, and they always have to wear a scarf…" Larry chuckled.

"No, it's weird; ;Evelina's skin is flawless."

"She's loaded, so I still say it's all bollocks and she's got a good surgeon." Larry came in closer to the stove and kissed her. "Trudi doesn't like stir fry; we'll have to go through the whole sore foot routine again tonight."

"I can't give her chocolate every evening; she's got to learn to eat savoury foods."

"I know that, but it's getting on my tits."

"You and me both." Ginny opened the oven to check on the progress of a tray of falafels.

"Can I get on *your* tits instead?" Larry's hands strayed to the front of her t-shirt.

"No; bugger off."

"Spoilsport."

CHAPTER 5

'DEAR MRS FORD, *thank you for sending us a sample of your material. However, unfortunately our lists are full and we are not taking on any new clients at this current time. We wish you every success with your writing career.'*

Ginny deleted the email as soon as she read the word 'unfortunately', and added it to a long list of similarly depressing emails. She sighed and sat back in her chair.

What was the use of trying just one more agent? They always sent back the same stock answer. With the cumulative amount of success she had been wished with her writing career by all these supercilious bastards, she should have been a bestselling author by now...........

Had she put too much 'heavy petting' into her novel? Isn't that what teens did? Or was that too old fashioned these days? Were they all at it whilst still at school as Evelina had intimated? The reality was they probably were, but the agents didn't seem to want 'it' written about in a Young Adult novel.

Perhaps she should change the genre? Make the protagonist five years older? Then the heavy petting wouldn't be enough; she'd have to be at it like rabbits with the lantern-jawed hero......

She might have to re-write the whole bloody novel!

Tired and disillusioned, Ginny looked up at the clock before switching off the computer. *Perhaps she should just stick to cleaning whilst Trudi was still young, and give up writing; she was surely earning more money from the Vecks than from selling any of her books on Amazon.*

Stretching and yawning, she wandered into the kitchen for a final cup of coffee before the school run. By concentrating so much on her novel she suddenly realised she had forgotten to turn the oven on for the casserole. *Tutting* with annoyance on also finding out that she had forgotten to prepare the casserole in the first place, Ginny grabbed a paring knife, some skinless chicken from the fridge and a selection of vegetables, and chopped and peeled for all she was worth. After boiling the kettle and adding some stock to the pot, she quickly shoved the casserole in the oven, tied her trainers, and made it to the school playground with only a few minutes to spare.

"Hello Mummy. I've made you a picture." Trudi ran up to her brandishing an A4 sized sheet of paper.

"That's lovely, darling." Ginny reluctantly dragged her mind away from her literary characters and concentrated on the grey piece of sugar paper in front of her.

"It's me, you and Daddy. I did a bigger one for Mrs Wright, and she put it on the wall. Can Tom come to tea?"

"Not today. Mummy's put a casserole in the oven now, and it won't stretch to four."

"I don't like casserole."

"So what's new?" Ginny sighed and picked up her daughter's lunch box.

"Why can't you cook something nice, like Tom's mum does?"

"What does she cook then?" Ginny followed behind Trudi as she ran to the exit gate.

"Pizza and chips."

"Tell you what; if you eat the casserole tonight, I'll get some pizzas for tomorrow and Tom can come over."

"Yippee! I don't like ham and pineapple pizza though." Trudi wrinkled her nose as Ginny rolled her eyes to the heavens.

CHAPTER 6

'SORRY; WILL BE late. It's a pigsty here. I don't know what went on last Friday night, but it'll take me forever to clear up. They've left me another £20 in the kitchen though."

Ginny received an almost instantaneous reply.

'The drinks are on you then. It's all under control. Trudi's got another gob on about eating a boiled egg and soldiers.'

She chuckled at Larry's Liverpudlian vernacular that only came to the fore when he was under stress. Putting the phone back in her coat pocket, she placed the note in her purse, and then unlocked the housekeeping cupboard. Finding a roll of black sacks still in place from the previous Friday, she tore off a couple and started towards the conference room, scooping up uneaten pizza crusts and dried up chips that had been scattered all over the table top. She then went from room to room emptying all the rubbish bins. As if by magic, the lift door opened as she struggled back down the corridor with two full bags.

"Hi Will. Good timing; sorry, got lots of rubbish for you today." She smiled at the concierge.

"I don't mind, it's all in a day's work." Will heaved the two sacks onto his shoulders like a modern-day Santa Claus, and disappeared back into the lift.

Donning her rubber gloves, she began work in the men's lavatories. She poured some bleach down into the toilet bowl in the first cubicle, but as she bent over to retrieve the toilet brush her gaze strayed to a small rectangular-shaped object that had fallen down inside the brush holder. Taking off her gloves she picked it up from the lid which was sticking out of the holder, turned it over, and read '2GB Lexar' on the front. Realising it was somebody's memory stick, she put it in the pocket of her overall, but then promptly forgot about it as she went about her duties.

After she had put Trudi to bed later that evening she sorted clothes for the washing machine, and was surprised to retrieve the memory stick still lodged in the top pocket of her dirty overall. She held it up to show her husband, standing at the other end of the kitchen.

"Look what I found today in the men's toilets. I forgot all about it until just now."

"A memory stick?"

"Yeah; I don't know who it belongs to though."

"Pop it in the computer and have a look. You never know, it might hold the secret formula to the elixir of youth, and I'll get the scoop of the century. I'm fed up of writing about old ladies' cats stuck up trees and school concerts." Larry chuckled and walked towards her.

"I can't; that'll be snooping; I'll just give it to one of the Misters. It's somebody's private property."

"Well, you won't know who it belongs to until you have a look will you? Give it to me; I'm a journalist and snooping's my business." He took the memory stick from her outstretched hand.

"You can't!"

"I can; just you watch me…" Larry held the memory stick and waved it about in the air.

"Hang on then; let me put the washing machine on and then I'll come and have a look with you."

Her heart started beating a little faster as Larry switched on the computer and plugged in the memory stick. When he opened the files they saw ten folders, all bearing boys' names.

"I don't recognise any of the names on these folders." Ginny shook her head while scanning files entitled, Zac, Ethan, Aiden, and Michael.

"I'll open 'Michael' and see if that helps." Larry clicked on the folder. "Fuckin' hell!" He exhaled forcefully and sat back. "Christ! We haven't got the elixir of youth, we've got the defilers of youth."

"Oh, God; this is sick." Ginny wanted to cry. "I recognise the background. The boy is lying on the sofa in Randolph Veck's office. I know that clock on the wall behind the sofa; it's Randolph's clock."

"Who's the boy?" Larry clicked through more naked pictures of the child taken from every conceivable angle.

"I don't know. Neither of the brothers have got any children, and nor has Evelina. Mr Charles' children are all grown up. The poor kid's even younger than Trudi. Larry; we have to take this to the police."

"Sure thing. Let's see if there's anybody else you recognise in the photos."

Larry clicked on a folder entitled 'All Together':

"This is the conference room. Now I know why there's so many pizzas in the freezer and why the room is left in such a state. These children are obviously brought there, fed, and then probably given money or presents in return for having God knows what done to them. Hang on, go back. There's somebody in the background in that one."

Larry returned to the previous photo for Ginny to scrutinise.

"Who is he, love? Have you seen him?"

"No, but I'd recognise him again if I saw him. He's etched into my brain now." She wanted to smash the supercilious grin off the man's face as he performed an act of sodomy. "Jesus; we've got to look at all of these now to find out if there's anyone I recognise. This is sick; sick." She sighed and put her head in her hands.

"We've got the scoop of the century here, babe." Larry's voice sounded upbeat. "We'll go to the police first thing in the morning. We've got the evidence here in our hands to nail these bastards."

A sudden thought struck Ginny like a bolt of lightning.

"Somebody's probably turning the offices upside down looking for this."

"I'll make a copy of all these photos and put them on another memory stick to keep here as insurance. We'll take another copy to the police. Take the original one back tomorrow and put it back where you found it. You know nothing, you've seen nothing, and you say nothing. You're three wise monkeys all on your own." Larry continued clicking through the photos. "Who are these guys?"

Ginny peered at the screen.

"It's Randolph and Dennis Veck, two of the directors. We've got a bombshell here Larry, I'm frightened. What if they find out and get to us or even Trudi?"

"Nobody's going to get to any of us as long as I'm alive."

"I've got to pretend that nothing's happened. I've got to go to work as usual. How the hell am I going to face them?"

"You do your work as quickly as possible and leave. I'll drop Trudi off at school, tell my boss what's going on, and then we'll go to the police together."

"I'm scared, Larry. These men are rich and powerful. They're going to fight back."

"We'll have the police and the newspaper behind us. They can't win." He put an arm around her shoulders, kissed the top of her head, and clicked on a file entitled 'Zac':

"Christ!" Larry sat up in the chair at the sight of a small boy with dark hair and sad eyes of the bluest blue, who was tied with rope to one of the chairs in the conference room.

"Oh, the poor little thing!" Ginny sobbed tears of outrage.

"It's not the child, although that's bad enough. It's the guy in the background."

She peered past the boy to focus on a naked man standing behind the boy's chair.

"I don't recognise him."

"I do." Larry put his head in his hands. "That's Mike Farnes, Editor of our newspaper."

CHAPTER 7

GINNY SLID THE memory stick back into the toilet brush holder the next day, soon after arriving in the building. Not a soul was about on the directors' corridor, and she lost no time in rushing through with the duster, polish, and vacuum cleaner, finishing her work by eight o'clock. She remembered to wave in Will's direction as she hurried towards the disabled exit.

"You're done early today." Will raised an arm and grinned.

"Doesn't need much cleaning on a Tuesday." She shrugged her shoulders.

"See you tomorrow."

"Yeah; bye Will."

Sitting in the passenger seat of the car while Larry drove to the school, Ginny listened to her daughter's chattering with half an ear as she prepared herself for the police interview. She checked that her memory stick with copies of the photos on was still in her jacket pocket, and waited impatiently at the school gates for the nine o'clock bell.

Satisfied on seeing the children disappear into the school building, Ginny made her way back to the car.

"It's now or never. Let's get it over with."

"Sure thing, babe." Larry pulled away from the kerb as her heart began beating a faster rhythm in her chest. "I'll leave the car in Sainsbury's car park; we'll never get in the High Street one, not even this time in the morning."

"I'm shaking."

"I'll be with you; don't worry."

They crossed the main road and headed towards the police station at the end of the street. Ginny checked yet again in her pocket to confirm that the memory stick was still there, and held it in her hand as they ran lightly up the steps. A bored-looking policewoman was on desk duty.

"Good morning. May I help you?" The smile was semi-sincere, and Ginny imagined how the woman's expression might change when discovering the reason for their visit.

"We need to speak to the duty Sergeant please." Ginny felt breathless with nerves, and was glad of Larry's solid presence.

"He's interviewing at the moment, but if you would like to wait he won't be much longer. Do you have an appointment?" The policewoman yawned and looked down at her diary.

"No; we'll wait." Larry's impatience with the woman's *ennui* made itself known in his curt reply.

"I'll take your details and then you can have a seat over there." She gestured with one hand to a bench in the corner of the foyer. "You're welcome to use the tea and coffee machine while you wait."

"We're Laurence and Virginia Ford; eighty four Grove Gardens, Arlborough."

"Thank you Mr Ford, you and your wife are next in the queue." The policewoman scribbled something in the diary.

With the wind taken out of her sails somewhat, Ginny sunk down onto the bench and fished around in her handbag for some change.

"It's my round; tea or coffee?" Larry was finding it difficult to settle, and was grateful for something to do.

"No more coffee; I'm wired enough already. Just tea please."

As soon as her hands had clamped around the warm polystyrene cup, the door to the interview room opened and Ginny saw a middle aged woman emerge who was drying her eyes with a handkerchief. Closely following behind her was a stolid-looking grey-haired man in his early forties, who wore the uniform of a sergeant. He spoke softly to the woman, who sniffed, nodded, and then made her way towards the exit. Ginny then briefly made eye contact with the sergeant before he glanced down at the desk diary.

"Mr and Mrs Ford; would you come this way please?"

Ginny stood up and followed Larry as he strode purposefully towards the sergeant. Entering the interview room she had a quick glance around, but could see nothing other than a large desk and four chairs in the centre of the room, a cupboard in one corner, and a side table holding a kettle, some mugs, and a box of teabags.

"I'm Sergeant Telford. Take a seat; how can I help you this morning?"

"Basically, my wife has found a memory stick that incriminates Randolph and Dennis Veck, two of the directors of PhizzFace beauty products, and also Mike Farnes, Editor of the Arlborough Standard, amongst unknown others." Larry exhaled with the relief of sharing his burden.

Sergeant Telford produced a small voice recorder from a drawer in the desk.

"Mrs Ford; I'm going to ask you a few questions. I hope you don't mind if I record this interview?"

"Not at all." Ginny shook her head and looked at Larry, who shrugged his shoulders.

The sergeant switched on the voice recorder and spoke into it with the date and time of the interview.

"Can we start with your name and address please."

"Virginia Ford, eighty four Grove Gardens, Arlborough."

"Do you have the memory stick in your possession?"

"Yes; it's here." Ginny took it from her pocket and placed it on top of the desk.

"Where did you find it?"

"Inside a toilet brush holder when I was cleaning the men's lavatories on the Phizzface directors' corridor." Her mouth felt dry with nerves, and she took a sip of tea.

"What is the address of Phizzface please?"

"Twenty eight to thirty five High Street, Arlborough."

"Have you looked at the contents of the memory stick?"

"Yes; I know I shouldn't have done it, but I wanted to try and find out who it belonged to so that I could give it back."

"What did you see?"

"Child abuse. Randolph and Dennis Veck are definitely paedophiles, along with Mr Farnes of the Arlborough

Standard and other men we don't recognise. There are photos of children being abused in PhizzFace's conference room, and also in Randolph Veck's office. These men *must* be arrested. Children are suffering because of them, and as far as I can tell this goes on most Friday afternoons; well, I suppose probably evenings actually when everybody has gone home. They keep stocks of food there in the freezer that children like to eat." Ginny felt elated at getting all the information out in the open. She took another swig of tea and sat back in her chair.

There was complete silence in the interview room as Sergeant Telford assimilated the information. The voice recorder was silent, deftly picking up the sound of a ticking clock on the wall above the kettle. Finally the sergeant cleared his throat as he reached over to grab the memory stick.

"Mrs Ford, I will take this memory stick personally to Chief Inspector Greensmith. Don't worry; if what you say is true, the men involved will be arrested forthwith. Please leave a statement at the desk outside. End of interview at ten hundred hours." He picked up the voice recorder, switched it off and then stood up, holding out his right hand: "Thank you for bringing this to our attention. The matter will be dealt with promptly."

"Thanks for listening." Ginny shook his hand and watched as Larry did the same.

"You'll be hearing from us soon." The sergeant made his way to the door and opened it.

"Goodbye." Ginny smiled at him as she walked out of the interview room.

CHAPTER 8

ON THE WEDNESDAY morning she zipped around the empty offices in record time; not a speck of dust had dared show its face. She noticed straight away that the memory stick had disappeared from its hiding place in the toilet brush holder. After her duties were completed, Ginny smoothed any imaginary creases from her overall and rapped on her manager's door with her knuckles.

"Come in!" Bob Fenton's voice could just be heard above the din coming from the factory floor above.

"Hi Bob; you wanted to see me?" Ginny turned the handle and stepped into the office.

"Come and sit down."

Ginny sensed that suddenly all was not well. Bob seemed on edge, and his voice was unusually without any humour whatsoever.

"Ginny; I'm sorry to say that I've had some complaints about your work." Bob looked awkward and ill at ease as he spoke.

"Complaints? What have I done?" Her heart started thudding in her chest.

"Miss Evelina says you have smashed one of her ornaments, and Mr Randolph and Mr Dennis say that you are taking too long to do the work, and that you are too noisy after nine o'clock. They say the toilets are filthy, and all the cups and plates have not been washed up properly."

Ginny was dumbfounded. For a moment she was unable to say a word, but then thought of a reply that she hoped would save the day.

"Truly I have never broken any of Miss Evelina's ornaments. I've also never had anything but praise from them. Why do they keep giving me twenty pound tips then, and telling me they're very pleased with my work?"

"I don't know, Ginny. All I do know is that they don't want you working for the company any more. I'm afraid I'm going to have to dispense with your services."

The July sun shone through the window, the birds sang in the trees outside, and Ginny's world suddenly came crashing down about her ears.

"You're giving me the sack? Bob; tell me this is a joke!" She fought back tears that threatened to cascade down her cheeks.

"Sorry; no joke. Please leave your overall here and collect your things from your locker. I have your P45 and half a week's wages all ready for you." He held out a small brown envelope.

As though in a dream, Ginny walked back to her locker. Her bag and jacket were still where she had put them at the start of the morning when she had still been a valued

PhizzFace employee. She was now without a job, and what was more, with no good reference recommending her, she would be without the means to gain another one. As she walked past the fountain in the foyer, even Will avoided her eye. She opened the disabled exit and walked through with her head held high.

The tears hit her as she turned her key in the front door. Without even taking off her jacket she gave in to her sorrow, crumpled into a ball on the bottom stair, hugged her knees, and rocked back and forth. Larry's voice coming out of nowhere startled her.

"Whatever's wrong love?"

"What are you still doing here? Haven't you taken Trudi to school?" Her voice came in hiccups as she wiped her eyes on a tissue and looked up at him.

"Of course I have. What's happened?" He joined her on the step and put his arm around her.

"Something at work; I've been sacked. Bob says my work's no good." The admission brought fresh tears to her eyes.

"You and me both. I'm angry as hell. I'm not going to let them get away with it. You know why we've been sacked, don't you?"

"Not you as well?" She looked at him incredulously.

"Think about it Ginny. We went to the police yesterday, and today we're both sacked. What does that tell you?"

She did not want to face the reality of it. Putting off the evil moment a bit longer, she sighed and blew her nose.

"I don't know."

"Yes you do. Sergeant Telford went to the chief inspector, who obviously alerted the Veck brothers and Mike Farnes straight away. They're not going to be prosecuted,

Ginny. The Vecks are no doubt paying off the police and Mike Farnes to shut them up; the cops and Mike are in on it as well."

The enormity of their plight began to sink in. Ginny put her head in her hands.

"What are we going to do? How are we going to live with no income?"

Larry gave her a squeeze.

"First things first; I'll go to the building society and ask if we can have a few months' grace on our mortgage until I can find another job. We can also get in touch with Social Services and let them know what's going on, and I've got a few contacts on the nationals; one especially owes me a favour. Then we've got to get away from here for a while; the schools break up soon, and the only people who have enough room for us are your mum and dad. You'll have to phone and ask if we can stay with them. I don't trust Farnes and those Veck bastards all the time they know that we know their dirty little game."

"Of course! That's why Emma went!" Ginny's blood ran cold for a moment.

"What?"

"Emma suddenly moved out, remember? She must have discovered something as well."

"Or they bumped her off."

"No; she moved out. Her neighbour said she had the chance of a better life."

The mystery of her friend's disappearance now began to make sense. Ginny wondered how they could ever win against such rich, powerful, and ruthless men. She spent the rest of the morning in a kind of daze, still unbelieving and hoping it had all been a bad dream. However, she was unaware that the reality of the situation would soon make itself apparent in the most terrible way imaginable.

CHAPTER 9

"I'VE MADE AN appointment for us at the Social Services department tomorrow, and I've left a voicemail message with a guy I know who works for one of the big national newspapers. He's straight as a dye; he won't let me down. I gave him a glowing reference a few years' back when he applied for the job he's got now." Larry looked up from the computer and gave Ginny a weak smile.

Ginny looked at the clock.

"It's time to get Trudi. Are you coming or not?" She picked up her purse and mobile phone, and put them in her bag.

"No; I've got some emails to send. I've got to carry on trying to find some more work."

The beautiful day outside belied the winter in her heart. Ginny walked along Grove Gardens trying to come to terms with everything that had happened in such a short space of time. She was lost in thought and by the time she reached the school some of the mothers were already walking away with their children. She hurried into the playground, glancing as she did so towards the exit door where the tardiest children were still dawdling out.

"Hi Ginny!" Ella Osborne held her son Tom's hand and waved with the other.

"Hey Ella, Tom's out early today for a change!"

"Yeah; he's got a dentist appointment. I told him he'd better be out on time or else!"

Ginny looked down at the little boy.

"Hi Tom! Is Trudi still in the classroom?" She looked towards the door again.

"No; she went away after we had our lunch." Tom yawned and dropped his lunchbox.

"Pick it up Tom; come on, we'll be late." Ella chided her son, not really hearing his words.

"What did you say, Tom?" Ginny knew that the boy could not be telling the truth, but all the same, his words had started a panicky feeling inside.

"An old lady was waiting at the gate at dinnertime. She asked me which one was Trudi Ford and I told her. She said she was Trudi's granny, and she said she had to take her to see her mummy in hospital. She had blue nails and lots of jewels on."

The boy's description struck a chord in Ginny's brain. She knew of only one person who possessed blue fingernails and lots of jewels.

Evelina!

Panic-stricken, Ginny looked towards the exit door for reassurance, but no other children were coming out, and her daughter was nowhere in sight.

"Oh my God, Ella! Trudi's been kidnapped!" Ginny looked wildly about the playground, but all the mothers were heading towards the gate with their offspring.

"Surely not! Tom, are you lying again?" Ella looked at her son sternly.

"No! Trudi got in the old woman's car! I saw her!" Tom looked close to tears.

"Was there a dinner lady on duty in the playground, Tom?" Ginny tried to think straight and calm the rising terror in her chest.

"Yes, but Mark Allsop and Darren Brown kept on fighting and Mrs Ogden had to take them to Mr Frinton."

"I'm sure she's inside Ginny; Trudi's too sensible to get in somebody's car."

Ella Osborne's reassuring words fell on deaf ears. Running faster than she had ever run before in her life, Ginny cleared the playground in two seconds flat. The usual warm end-of-the-day smell of stuffy classrooms, stale cabbage and crayons enveloped her as she made her way to classroom 3a at the end of the corridor. She saw Trudi's painting on the wall outside the classroom, the one she had not listened to her daughter chattering on about; the one entitled 'My Family', where Trudi had painted herself standing safely in-between her mummy and daddy. There and then Ginny made a promise to herself to never listen to her daughter again with only half an ear.

Where was she?

Ginny could see only the teacher still at her desk, quietly marking books.

"Mrs Wright; have you seen Trudi?" Her legs had turned to jelly, and a queasy feeling had settled in the pit of her stomach.

"No, Mrs Ford; I was informed after lunch by Mrs Ogden that Trudi had been collected by her grandmother because of a family crisis."

The teacher's look of concern tipped Ginny over the edge. She sank tearfully down on one of the child-size tables, bereft, dazed, and despondent.

"Why did nobody keep an eye on my little girl? She's been kidnapped!" Ginny wailed wildly, unable to control her emotions.

"I'm so sorry, Mrs Ford; we were told she was with her grandmother."

"Her grandmother lives three hundred miles away!"

"I'll call the police right now!" The teacher reached for a mobile phone in her bag.

"No! It's no use phoning the police; I know who took her!" Ginny's words came through heaving sobs, as she wiped her eyes and tried to think straight.

"All the more reason to tell the police."

"I will; I shall go there straight away, but I'm also going to make a complaint to the council. Mrs Ogden should be sacked." She rose from the table and headed towards the door.

"Do you want me to come with you?"

"No, I'm fine; really."

"Well, if you're sure…" The teacher looked as though she wanted to be somewhere else.

Her mobile phone rang as Ginny made her way across the empty playground. She saw Larry's name displayed on the screen.

"Evelina Veck took Trudi from the playground at lunchtime!" Her words still sounded shaky with grief.

"I know; she's just phoned here. She says no Police and no Press. She's going to contact us tonight. Apparently Trudi is being well looked after and she's unharmed.

I want to rip out her heart! The fucking evil bitch!" Larry's voice rose in anger. "I'm coming to the school now! They're going to pay for this!"

"Leave it Larry; they can't do anything. I'm going to make a complaint against the dinner lady, for what good it'll do. I'm coming home now. We'll have to wait for the Vecks to get in touch." She was more in control now, and somehow felt ready to face whatever was coming her way.

Ginny kept her eyes downcast, spoke to nobody, and ran along Arcadia Road. When she turned into Grove Gardens she could see Larry hurrying towards her. She ran into his arms and they held each other silently on the pavement, as all around them women carrying brightly coloured lunchboxes walked their chattering children home from school.

CHAPTER 10

"WHEN WILL SHE be contacting us again?"

Ginny sat by the phone, willing it to ring. She watched as Larry paced backwards and forwards, wearing a slight groove in the carpet with his feet.

"I don't know. Tonight; that's all she said, apart from the bit about not going to the police. If they've hurt Trudi they'll have to look over their shoulder for the rest of their miserable lives, 'cos I'll be gunning for them." Larry paced to the window and looked out.

"Do you want any dinner? I can't eat a thing, but I'll cook something for you if you like." Ginny sighed and looked at her watch; the hands showed 5:55pm.

"No, love; it's okay. I'm not hungry."

"I've felt sick since Trudi's been gone. It doesn't seem to be going away."

"Me as well; angry too. Bloody tear-the-Vecks-apart angry. I want to…kill the fuckers!" Larry looked left and right along the street through the net curtains. "They've got us just where they want us!" He kicked the wall as hard as he could.

"Where did you put that memory stick?" Ginny's brain started to race.

"It's in the desk. Why?"

"They know where we live from PhizzFace's personnel records. They'll know we gave the police a copy because I put the original one back where I found it. They could send someone here to turn the place upside down if they think we've copied another one." Panic started to wash over her again.

"I'll put it in a plastic bag and bury it somewhere in the garden. It's our only weapon against them. We've got to keep it safe." Larry, pleased at being able to do something, stopped pacing and made his way along to the study.

Ginny flopped back on the sofa and closed her eyes. The house was too quiet without Trudi. Right now she suddenly ached to be helping her daughter with her reading; filling in the homework book, and listening to Trudi complain about having to do homework when all her friends were watching TV. She felt impotent, and railed against the hopelessness of the situation.

In the stillness she must have dozed off. When Larry came back into the front room she awoke with a start and looked at her watch again. Another half an hour had flown by in a flash.

"I've wrapped it in a bin liner and buried it under the rhubarb leaves; we're not overlooked in that bit of the garden. I wasn't seen. Nobody will ever think of looking for it there." He paced to the window again and looked out.

"Come and sit down with me, I could do with a bit of a cuddle."

"Yeah, sorry."

Ginny wrapped her arms around him and rested her head on his shoulder. They sat in silence, lost in their own thoughts for a while.

"Do we tell Mum and Dad or your sisters?" Ginny worried about the effect that their granddaughter's disappearance would have on her elderly parents.

"No; not yet. It's best we tell nobody until we have Trudi back. Then we can go to maybe Social Services or the Childline people." Larry sighed. "The trouble is, we don't know where the kids have come from."

"We'll have to spy on the building one Friday night, follow them, and see where the kids are taken back to."

"Yeah, that can be done; I can sit in the car and wait for them to come out, but they'll probably alter the venue now that we know what's going on."

"Yeah; it's hopeless. They've got the upper hand every which way." Ginny stood up and prowled around the room like a caged tiger. "I'm so scared they'll hurt Trudi, and I can't do a bloody thing about it." She looked at the phone again.

"Come and sit down."

"I can't." She went over to the window. "Larry………..! There's a car pulling up outside!"

In a trice Larry was standing beside her.

"Who is it?"

"It's Evelina!"

Ginny stood and watched as if in a trance, as the familiar figure of a bejewelled and expensively dressed older woman stepped neatly out of the driver's seat of a dark blue BMW, opened their garden gate, and made her way slowly up the path.

"I'll kill the fucking bitch!" Larry made to turn for the door.

"No! Stay here love; we need to keep calm. She hasn't got Trudi with her. I'll let her in and see what she's got to say."

She could hardly hear the doorbell ring over her thudding heart. She managed to keep her face expressionless as she turned the handle of the front door and faced her daughter's kidnapper.

"Good evening, Ginny. I take it you've told nobody?" Evelina Veck stepped briskly into the passageway without any invitation.

"Nobody knows." Ginny shook her head. "Where is my daughter? What have you done with her?" She held Larry's hand as he joined her in the hallway, stony faced and breathing heavy with rage.

"When you have signed my proposal, Trudi will be dropped off here unharmed and unhurt. In fact, for your information she has had a lovely afternoon at the beach. I'm sure she will tell you all about her day when she sees you."

Evelina's gaze was mesmerising, and Ginny found herself staring unblinkingly into two icy grey eyes that seemed devoid of any emotion whatsoever.

"May I come inside so that we can sit down? I would like to discuss my proposal with you."

"Come this way please."

Ginny, holding on to Larry's hand in an attempt to keep him calm, led the way back to the front room. She pulled out three chairs from under the dining table.

"Sit down. We want to hear what you have got to say."

"Whatever it is, it had better be quick. I want you out of my house and my daughter back." Larry took his hand from Ginny's, sat down heavily, and folded his arms.

"All in good time." Evelina took out a small folder from her bag. "I've had our solicitors draw up this agreement today. I'm going to explain it to you, and then you can have a read through it before you sign."

"What makes you think I'm going to sign it?" Larry shot a glance at Evelina.

"Mr Ford; we are very rich and powerful people. I'm sure you will want to sign it when you've read it." Evelina took out a silver coloured fountain pen and laid it down next to the folder.

"So......explain then." Larry looked Evelina straight in the eyes, sat back in his chair, and waited.

CHAPTER 11

GINNY PERCHED ON the edge of her seat as Evelina cleared her throat and took her time.

"As you know, when he was a young man my brother Randolph found the answer to reverse ageing and wrinkled skin. This made Randolph, and eventually Dennis and myself multi-millionaires. There is no other family member left alive apart from cousin Rupert, and we are extremely wealthy.

"Rub my nose in it a bit more; I'm sure you're getting a great kick out of this." Larry exhaled forcefully, sat back in his chair and crossed his legs.

Ignoring the interruption, Evelina carried on.

"Randolph and Dennis were sent off to boarding school at a very early age. They told me years later about the 'procedures' that they were forced to endure after the lights were turned out. Those nights of terror year in and year out, made them the men they are today."

"So what you're saying is that because they were buggered by the other boys, it turned them into paedophiles for the rest of their lives?" Larry, shrugging his shoulders, sat forward in his seat; never taking his eyes from Evelina's painted face.

"Not the boys, Mr Ford; the masters. The masters turned my brothers away from the straight and narrow. They were singled out because of Randolph's beauty and intelligence. Dennis was forced into complicity simply because he was Randolph's sibling."

"So why didn't they speak up and report the teachers?"

"Who would have believed them? A child is powerless in the face of such cruelty. Instead the injustice simmered, and when he grew up Randolph especially vowed never to be in a position of extreme powerlessness and subjugation again."

"No; he and his brother decided to inflict the same suffering on other innocent kids instead, because they can." Larry sighed and shook his head. "You Vecks are something else."

Ginny saw Evelina glance away from Larry and towards her.

"Mrs Ford; I trust your husband is not going to keep interrupting me?"

Ginny grabbed her husband's hand again, and looked at the folder on the table.

"He's listening; the same as me."

"Very well. I'll carry on." Evelina uncrossed and re-crossed her legs, and cleared her throat again.

"The sexual practises that my brothers were forced to endure from the age of about seven years old until they were well into their teens, made them immune to any commonly called 'normal' sexual behaviour. The dye was cast, so to speak." Evelina paused for breath.

"So what have these two perverts done to my daughter?" Larry's impatience was beginning to make itself felt.

"Absolutely nothing, I can assure you. Have you been listening to me? Girls do not interest either Randolph or Dennis. Your daughter has been to the beach today with myself and a family friend. My friend will bring her back to you in approximately one hour."

"So what have *you* done to her, you sick fucking bitch?" Larry pounded his fist on the table.

"Larry; hear her out! They're bringing Trudi back soon." Ginny tried to calm the underlying tension around the table.

Evelina sighed with impatience as she addressed Larry.

"I've never had any children of my own. I enjoyed an innocent afternoon with a child. It just so happened to be *your* child. We played sandcastles on the beach, ate ice cream, and Trudi had fish and chips for supper and a pony ride afterwards. I not only work for PhizzFace; I work for my brothers, and they keep me in the manner to which I have become accustomed. As I said before, they are extremely wealthy, and they usually get what they want. I help them to carry out their wishes."

"Which are?" Larry's fists uncurled and he intertwined his fingers.

"At the moment it is your silence and your wife's silence. I have been instructed by my brothers to offer you the sum of three million pounds. In return you will not contact the authorities; indeed the chief of police has ways to find out if you do. You are to forget everything that you know, perhaps move away from the area, and then carry on with your life as if we did not exist. Oh, and you are also to return to me any more copies of the memory stick that you may have made."

Ginny's jaw dropped with disbelief. Next to her she was aware that Larry had suddenly sat up straighter in his seat.

"And what if we don't want to sign?" Ginny looked up at the clock to work out when she could look forward to hearing her daughter's voice again.

"Then your daughter will not be returned to you. I must make one call in approximately fifteen minutes' time." Evelina opened the folder and took out a form, slid the pen and paper across the table, and then rummaged in her bag for her mobile phone.

The silence in the room was overwhelming. Sweat trickled down in rivulets from Larry's forehead onto his cheeks. The clock ticked away the minutes, and Ginny felt as though she was in some sort of trance. Finally she saw Larry looking at her, and she nodded.

"We'll sign." She reached for the form, added her signature, and then passed the piece of paper to her husband.

"Well done. I knew this little problem could be settled in no time at all!" Evelina spoke briefly into her phone, stood up, and held out her hand.

"Goodbye. We won't meet again."

"I won't shake your hand if you don't mind." Larry turned away.

"As you wish. Ginny's bank details are still with Personnel. Your money will be sent by bank transfer tomorrow. By the way, are you holding on to any other copies of the memory stick?"

"No. We gave our copy to the police."

CHAPTER 12

"I CAN'T SLEEP, can you?" Ginny whispered in the dark.

"No. Come over here and have a cuddle."

"Thank God Trudi's home. She didn't seem any the worse for her day out." Ginny shuffled over to Larry's side of the bed and put her head on his shoulder.

"She was telling me all about her pony ride. She wants a pony now, by the way." Larry put his arm around her shoulders.

"Well, it seems that after tomorrow we'll be able to buy her a whole stable full of horses." Ginny sighed. "The trouble is, it does nothing for the poor boys we set out to help."

"You heard the old witch; we've got to stay schtum."

"That's not the right thing to do though."

"I know, but when it comes to keeping my family alive, then that's what I *am* going to do. Think about it…. what would anyone else do under the same circumstances?" Larry gave her shoulder a little squeeze to reinforce his statement.

"Yeah, I suppose most people would do the same."

"There you go then."

"It still doesn't make it right."

"Yeah, but it makes it all right with me."

Ginny absent-mindedly twisted a strand of Larry's hair round and round in her fingers.

"It doesn't seem possible that they'll give us three million pounds just like that." Her brain still could not take in the enormous amount of money involved.

"They're as rich as Croesus. It's probably pocket money to them."

"What shall we do with it all?"

"Enjoy it for the rest of our lives." Larry chuckled.

"I feel so guilty.........those kids...." Ginny sighed again.

"It's a dog eat dog world. My old man was right when he told me to look after number one, and that's what I'm going to do. That's what *we're* going to do."

"I wish I could be like you." Ginny closed her eyes.

Larry sat up in bed, switched on the bedside lamp, and looked at her.

"Listen; most folks would give their eye teeth for three million pounds. We can afford to have more children; we can buy a big house in the country to bring them up in, and we can give them everything we never had ourselves."

"But can you live with yourself at the end of the day?" Ginny, irritatingly still wide awake, sat up and put one arm across his back.

"Too bloody right I can live with myself." He climbed out of bed. "Tell you what; I'll bring you back a cup of tea, and then we can have another cuddle."

Left alone, Ginny lay back on the pillows. She thought of four frightened, powerless boys having to go through hell every week, with no end to their suffering in sight. There and then she made a promise to herself that as soon as she could, by fair means or foul, she would find some way to help them.

PART 2 – ONE YEAR LATER

CHAPTER 13

GINNY LOOKED ON fondly as Larry executed a perfect somersault off the long diving board, disappearing into the pool's dark blue depths headfirst with barely a splash marring the surface. Trudi clapped enthusiastically from the safety of the shallow end as her father emerged by her side, rubbing the chlorine from his eyes.

"Do it again, Daddy!"

"That's enough for today; I'm not a performing seal! It's time you were getting ready for bed. It's school tomorrow." Larry hauled himself out, and stood bronzed and dripping on the edge of the pool.

"Why does Miss Argent have to come here? Why can't I go to school with other children like I used to?" Trudi climbed up the steps to join her father.

"There isn't a school nearby. I've already told you that." He put a towel around his daughter's shoulders and picked her up. "I love you so much that I want you here with me all the time!" He kissed the top of her head fondly. "Come on; I'll read you a story, and it's your turn to pick which one."

Ginny watched them disappear through the open patio doors, and then laid back on her lilo and floated around on the surface of the water. The evening sun was yet to sink below the horizon. Her son woke up and moved about inside her; she rested a hand on her abdomen and smiled at the white fluffy clouds as they swirled over her head in the gentle summer breeze. The heat of the day still hung in the air, making her feel heavy and lethargic. She closed her eyes.

"Wake up sleepyhead!"

She heard her husband's voice coming from afar, as the lilo moved under the weight of his arms.

"I must have dozed off. What's the time?" She looked at the horizon towards the setting sun.

"About quarter to nine. Trudi fell asleep eventually after twenty five pages of James and the Giant Peach. Your turn tomorrow." He smiled and kissed her.

She was suddenly wide awake, and slightly chilly.

"I'm cold." She put her arms around his neck and slid into the water.

"I'll warm you up." He put one hand around her waist and drew her to him. "Come here."

The water was still warm from the sun's rays, and took the chill from her body. His mouth found hers and she opened her lips to receive his tongue. Locked in an embrace, they moved towards a wall in the middle of the pool.

"I want you so much. You and Trudi are my world. I want to make many babies with you."

"I love you, Larry." She saw the longing in his eyes, matching her own sudden need.

He removed her bikini slowly. Feeling down in the water she slid off his trunks, throwing them aside to join her string bikini laying on the bottom of the pool. His penis felt engorged, and throbbed with desire. She arched her back as he licked her breasts, swollen with early pregnancy. Putting an arm in the drainage gulley on either side of her, she wrapped her weightless legs around him and closed her eyes with pleasure as she felt him enter her.

"I'll be careful; don't want to disturb junior." He put his hands under her buttocks and moved gently to and fro. She found his rhythm and shut out the world; creating a delicious tension by spreading her legs a little wider so that her feet rested on either side of his waist. When her climax came she moaned, tipped back her head, and felt his answering shudder a few seconds later.

"Jesus; you'll have to get pregnant more often. Twice a day suits me just fine!"

She wrapped her arms around his neck and pressed her cheek to his.

"It won't last. Make the most of it."

"I'm game if you are. Just give me ten minutes."

He nibbled her ear, making her shiver.

"I want to get out now; did Bridget leave us any clean towels in the changing room?"

"There's three left. Bags I the biggest one!" Larry hauled himself out and ran naked to the changing room.

"Our swimming costumes are still at the bottom of the pool! I'm not putting my head under to get them; I'll ruin my hair." Ginny climbed up the steps, pleased to be handed a warm towel off the rail.

"I'll get them tomorrow before Bridget comes back." Larry dried himself and wrapped the towel around his waist. "Steven will be making his rounds soon; we'd better get out, or we'll give him a bit of a shock. Let's go in and check on Trudi first, and then we can put a film on if you like."

"Yeah; sounds good."

Feeling less cold, Ginny followed Larry past the sun deck and then into the back lobby. Padding through the front entrance hall and up the grand staircase, they traversed the landing to the end where Trudi slept the sleep of the exhausted.

"All that swimming's worn her out." Ginny whispered and smiled fondly at their daughter.

Larry nodded as he put an arm around her shoulders.

"Pat Argent is going to have a devil of a job with her tomorrow. All she wants to do is swim."

"I sometimes look at her and all she has, and then think of those unfortunate kids in the conference room at PhizzFace." Ginny sighed, "Especially that one named Zac; poor little sod."

"We can't do anything about it; you know that." Larry tiptoed in and pulled the sheet over Trudi's sleeping body. "It'll put us all at risk again."

"Sometimes I can't sleep at night thinking about them." Ginny closed the bedroom door and shook her head. "There must be a way to save little Zac and all the others. We've still got a copy of the memory stick; we could research online for the best people to give it to."

"And get Trudi kidnapped again, or worse."

Ginny wracked her brain as they continued back down the landing to their bedroom.

"I know! How about if we hire a private detective?" She flopped down onto the bed and admired at her husband's muscular body as he let the damp towel fall to the floor. "The Vecks won't know he's working for us."

"I've thought about that in the past, but if they catch him and he talks, then it's curtains for us." Larry adopted a Tarzan-like stance and beat his chest with both fists, "Look out, I'm going to leap on you!"

Giggling, Ginny managed to turn away just at the right moment.

"No, I'm serious." She sat up and looked at him. "I just can't go on, living in this dream of a house and pretending everything's all right. I've got to try and do something to help those poor kids."

"You'll be making a big mistake. We can't help them. Our number one priority is keeping Trudi and the new baby safe." Larry pulled her to him. "Forget it, Ginny. We've got everything here we ever wanted, and more."

Temporarily mollified, she snuggled up to him.

"I love you, Larry."

"Love you too."

CHAPTER 14

"COME IN PAT; Trudi's already in the school room."

Ginny pressed the buzzer to open the main gates. On the security screen in the kitchen she saw Pat Argent's car move slowly down the driveway. The governess alighted stiffly from the Citroen 2V, and made her way to the main door. Ginny heard Bridget's lilting Irish welcome, and Miss Argent's clipped response.

"Good morning; Trudi's finishing off her essay for you." Ginny smiled as she stepped out into the hallway to greet her daughter's tutor.

"Good morning Mrs Ford. I wonder if I may have a word before I go along to Trudi?"

"Of course; come into the kitchen. Is there something the matter?" Ginny searched the older woman's face for any inkling of what could be wrong.

"No problem, but I was wondering if I could take Trudi to the museum in town? We're covering the Victorian era in class, and there's an exhibition there all this week of costumes and artefacts from the eighteen forties to the eighteen nineties."

Ginny's heart began to race at the thought of it.

"We do prefer her to stay in the school room, but if you really think it would be of benefit to her, then I'll get one of the security guys to accompany you. Which day were you thinking of going?" She hoped her terror had not shown itself during the conversation.

"Probably Wednesday if that's okay?"

"I'll check with Steven in a while before he goes off duty, and I'll let you know."

"Thank you." The governess turned towards the kitchen door.

Ginny sat down with a sigh on one of the breakfast bar stools and tried to concentrate on calming thoughts. When her heart had settled back to its normal rhythm she brewed some camomile tea and took it out onto the sun deck overlooking the pool, watching as her husband performed his usual perfect and mesmerising front crawl. Although it was only just after nine o'clock, she knew Larry had probably already completed an hour in the gym and had swum at least eighty lengths. The morning sun was warm on her face, heralding the start of another scorching day.

She turned around on recognising some heavy footsteps behind her.

"I'm just off now Mrs Ford. Leon's in the office today."

"Thanks Steven. Are you on a day shift at all on Wednesday?"

"Yes; this was the last night for a week." Steven Marshall tried hard to stifle a yawn.

"I'd like you to accompany Miss Argent and Trudi to the Arlborough museum on Wednesday. We'll need either Stuart or Andy to cover here while you're away. Would that be okay?"

"That's fine; I'll speak to Miss Argent tomorrow and find out the time when she wants to go."

"Thanks Steven." She checked on Larry, still swimming up and down. "By the way, would you know of any good private detectives?" She held her breath and hoped her voice had not carried across to the pool.

"I think Leon would know the answer to that one."

His questioning raise of the eyebrows was not lost on her. However, aware of Larry's friendship with the burly ex-bouncer, she decided that the less people knew of her intentions, the better it would be.

"I'll leave it in your capable hands then, but this is only between the two of us. Larry is not to know."

"Fair enough. I'll have a word with Leon then, and come back to you."

She relaxed as Steven's footsteps retreated around to the front of the house. The sun sparkled on Larry's tanned skin as he hauled himself out of the pool in one fluid movement.

"Hey! How's it going?" Dripping, he came over and sat beside her.

"Okay. I'll be off to the study in a minute to do some writing. I've started a novel loosely based what's been happening to us over this past year." She smiled at him and let her eyes linger on his well-developed musculature.

"I'm sure it'll be a bestseller; as long as you don't mention anyone's name though." Larry lifted his face to the sun and closed his eyes.

"No, of course not. What have you got on today?" She felt another throbbing in her groin as her gaze travelled down his body.

"I'm checking out a nightclub I'm thinking of taking over in town. Steven can get the staff. It's a job of sorts for me, and it'll be a good little earner for the future." He picked up a towel from the back of the chair and rubbed his hair. "I'll be back early afternoon." He stood up and threw the towel over his shoulders.

"Okay. Oh; Pat wants to take Trudi to the museum on Wednesday. Steven's going with them though."

"Fine; Pat's good with her. Trudi's coming on in leaps and bounds." He kissed her and ruffled the top of her head on his way in to the house. "See you later."

Ginny drained her cup and then made her way to the study, careful not to distract her daughter as she passed by the school room. Logging on, she retrieved her manuscript, and chewed the end of a pen for some time as she tried to think of a suitable title.

Paid off by Paedophiles?
The Only Millionaire Housekeeper in the World?
For the Sake of a Child?
Look Beneath the Surface?

Lost in thought, she failed to hear the first gentle tapping on the study door. It was only when the knocking increased and pervaded her thoughts that she was dragged back to reality. Her voice was louder than usual, showing irritation at the interruption.

"Come in!" She turned around unsmiling.

"Sorry to interrupt, Mrs Ford. Steven said you were looking for a private detective."

"Oh yes; come in Leon."

Feeling guilty for her curt manner towards the security guard, Ginny smiled, put down her pen, and swivelled around in her chair to face him.

"Do you know of somebody then?" She pulled out another chair from under the long teak desk that ran along one wall.

"My brother-in-law is a private investigator; very good at it as well." Leon's bulk seemed too big for the chair, which creaked under his weight as he sat down.

"Please tell him to get in touch by sending me a text to let me know when he is free to come here and discuss business. As he is recommended by you, it'll be okay to give him my mobile number. Did Steven tell you that Mr Ford is not to know?

"Yes. I won't say a word."

Ginny sensed he was waiting for more information.

"I'll look forward to hearing from him. What's his name?"

"Phil Desborough."

"Thanks Leon. That'll be all." She smiled again and scribbled on a piece of paper. "Here's the number to use; I'm grateful for your help."

CHAPTER 15

"THEY'RE NOT BACK yet. It's nearly four o'clock. What time did Pat say she'd be here? I'm going for a walk to see if they're coming up the driveway." Agitated, Ginny opened the main door.

"Steven is with them; don't worry." Larry quickened his pace to catch up with her. "We can always take a drive down to the museum ourselves if you're that concerned." He held her hand and they walked together.

"You know I'm frightened of leaving the estate. I can't do it." She felt close to tears.

"It's been a year; we haven't heard a thing from the Vecks. We've left them alone and they've done the same to us. You really ought to make an effort, Gin."

"I know; I just need more time, that's all." She scanned the driveway as she walked.

"What if we go to the supermarket in town tomorrow instead of having the food delivered? Pat will be with Trudi; we can take our time, and come back with the week's groceries." He looked at her hopefully.

"I haven't been shopping for ages. The trolleys are all chained up; I've forgotten if you have to put a pound in the handle thing first or not." Her heart was racing, and she felt an overwhelming anxiety at the thought of venturing beyond the high walls of their estate, but knew she could not stay a virtual prisoner for the rest of her life.

"We can work that out when we get there." He squeezed her hand. "What do you say?"

"I'll think about it after Trudi's home."

The tarmac felt hot under her sandals as they carried on down towards the main gate. The poplar trees lining either side of the driveway offered a small amount of shade, and Ginny tried to stay underneath their branches to escape the heat. As they neared the end of the driveway the gates began to open automatically and she saw their familiar dark blue Range Rover appearing, with Trudi waving at them from the back seat.

"There you are; I told you nothing's wrong. Steve's a good guy. You've got to start trusting people again."

Larry acknowledged the Range Rover as it edged slowly through the gates and then stopped. The electric window descended, and Ginny waved back to her daughter.

"Everything okay Steve?"

"Fine; no problems."

"I want to get out and walk with Mummy and Daddy!" Trudi unclipped her seat belt and stood up.

"Out you get then, Princess. Did you have a good day?" Larry opened the car door, kissed his daughter, and lifted her up onto his shoulders.

"It was the best, but Miss Argent made me answer loads of questions!"

"That's because it was a school trip. Miss Argent is supposed to do that." Larry winked at the governess sitting in the front seat. "See you tomorrow Pat."

"Goodbye Mr Ford." A sliver of a smile graced the tutor's lips.

The Range Rover carried on down the driveway, as Ginny and Larry turned back towards the house.

"Doesn't she ever unbend just a little bit?" Larry wrapped his arms around Trudi's lower legs and gave them a squeeze. "Hold tight Princess!"

"Leave her alone; she's an excellent teacher. Most parents would give their eye teeth to have the one-to-one that Trudi has. Look how far she's come in one year."

"I know Gin, but it's like someone's stuck a rod up......."

"Little people have big ears." Ginny interrupted and looked up at her daughter.

"I haven't got big ears!" Trudi's face registered complete revulsion.

"Mummy didn't mean it in that way. Would you like a swim with Daddy before dinner?"

"Woo-hoo! Hurry up Daddy! I want to get back to the house!"

"Wave nicely to Miss Argent then; she'll be driving out in a minute."

"Good."

"Now, now; that's not being very kind, is it?" Ginny looked away and tried hard not to laugh.

"She said I got one question wrong." Trudi waved as the Citroen went by.

"Out of how many?" Ginny raised a hand and acknowledged the governess.

"Millions."

"Well; I don't think that's too bad then. What do you think Daddy?" Ginny laughed and looked at Larry.

"I think my Princess is the bestest, cleverest little girl in the whole world!" Larry chuckled along with her and bounced his daughter up and down on his shoulders as they all walked back to the house.

The message she had been waiting for came later that night; Ginny heard her phone ping as they watched the ten o'clock news. She looked across at Larry; dozing and unaware of the incoming text. She picked up her phone from the coffee table and tapped in her password.

'This is Phil Desborough. I am free tomorrow 1 – 2pm. Let me know if convenient.'

Ginny's heart did a quick somersault and then a backflip. Larry would be out finalising the deal at the club. She knew that once she answered his text there would be no turning back. Tapping out a response, she re-read it before sending.

'1 o'clock is fine. Announce yourself at the gate through the intercom. Ginny Ford.'

CHAPTER 16

"MR DESBOROUGH; THANK you for coming along." Ginny held out her hand, which was clamped in a firm greeting by a well-built, dark haired man in his late forties.

"Call me Phil, but definitely not Philip; My mother's the only one who calls me Philip, and it winds me up every time. She knows I hate it; she does it on purpose."

Phil Desborough's booming voice sounded extra loud in the confines of the study. Ginny wondered if Steve Marshall could hear it as he sat monitoring the cameras near to the main door.

"Phil; Leon didn't say why you were needed; that's because he doesn't know. What I have to tell you will remain just between the two of us. My husband doesn't know I've called you, and if you do meet him by accident at some point you'll have to say that you're Leon's relative and one of Steve's new security men."

"Okay; I can do that. So; is it the usual?" Phil looked around the study as he spoke.

"The usual?" Ginny saw that he'd found their wedding photo and was gazing at it intently.

"You know; husband having an affair and all that."

"No, no. Well, not that I know of anyway." Ginny shrugged her shoulders.

"What then?"

Ginny was finding the investigator ever so slightly irritating. She went over to the open safe and took out a memory stick, conscious that his eyes were following her every move.

"This is the reason you are here. I have another copy in the safe, but on no account let it out of your sight." She placed the memory stick in his outstretched hand. "It contains photos taken about a year ago of children being abused by two paedophile directors at PhizzFace Inc, the beauty products' company in Arlborough High Street, and also by other people in authority; some of them are high up in the newspaper world and in the police force. I found out that the abuse takes place in the directors' offices upstairs, usually on Friday nights. I need you to find out where the children are being taken back to, and then we must find a way to contact the NSPCC or suchlike without the perpetrators discovering who shopped them. I'll not rest until these men are put away, but please do not act on what you find out without speaking to me first." She wiped away some tears and tried to stop her voice from shaking. "I'm four months' pregnant, so excuse me for being a bit emotional."

She heard Phil Desborough whistle softly.

"Wow; strong stuff then." He turned the memory stick over and over in his hands. "How on earth did you come by it?"

"I used to clean the offices; I found it in the men's toilets and looked at it to see who it belonged to so that I could give it back. They've no idea I made a copy." Ginny decided to leave out any other pertinent information.

"How come you live here but worked as a cleaner?" His face could not help but register surprise.

Ginny, trying to cover up the real truth, could have kicked herself for the mistake.

"I had to work at the time, but then we won the lottery. We decided, maybe wrongly, to stay near enough to Arlborough so that our daughter could still see her old schoolfriends. We love the beach and the shops, and it wasn't worth trying to find a better area to settle in; the police have ways to find us even if we had moved hundreds of miles away."

"The lottery, eh? I'll be all right for payment then!"

"Mr Desborough, I can assure you that your fee will be paid promptly." Ginny wished him gone as soon as ever she could get him out of the door.

"It's Phil don't forget. Why did you leave it so long before contacting me?"

"I don't know; probably because I couldn't live with my conscience anymore."

She watched him put the memory stick in the pocket of his trousers.

"Here's a list of my rates, and you have my number. You can call me any time; day or night. I'll be in touch as soon as I have an answer for you." He handed her a well-thumbed piece of paper.

As she walked him back to the entrance hall she saw Steve Marshall lift his head briefly from the security screens, but again decided it would be better to discuss the situation with as few people as possible. She followed the investigator through the main door and out onto the driveway, noticing waves of heat shimmering above the roof of his Volvo.

"It's going to be hot in there when you open the door." She smiled and shook his hand.

"No worries; that's why God created air-conditioning."

His grip was too firm and his hand was sweaty. Ginny released her fingers and watched him drive away with a sigh of relief, deciding to walk up to the gate to meet Larry in case he was on his way home from the club.

Not a breath of wind moved the branches of the trees. Even the birds were silent; their energy seemingly sapped in the summer heat. As Ginny arrived at the intercom the gates had just closed, but a sudden urge to be rid of constant anxiety and to venture out beyond the suffocating confines of the high walls overcame her and she picked up the phone.

"Hi Steve; can you open the gate again for me please? I'm going to walk a bit; Larry will be coming home soon and I'll grab a lift back."

"Are you sure, Mrs Ford?" The voice in her ear registered concern.

"I'm fine; please open the gate."

Her heart began to race as the huge security gates unlocked to reveal the world outside. Ginny had all but forgotten about the leafy country lane leading up to the estate, which seemed empty of traffic and pleasantly shady. She made a right turn and started to walk in the direction of Arlborough town, stepping up onto the verge if she could hear any cars approaching.

Insects flew overhead, and her heartbeat slowed with the relaxing pace. After about 20 minutes of walking she stopped by a stile to take in the peaceful view of a field of cows munching mechanically. Their limpid brown eyes observed her from afar as their jaws worked ceaselessly to chew the cud; flies buzzed and droned around the cows' eyes. In the distance a combine harvester effortlessly completed work a team of Shire horses in previous times would have taken days to finish. Ginny leaned on the stile in a happy dream; pleased that she had finally managed to conquer her fear of venturing past the estate's walls.

A screeching of tyres behind her caused her to snap out of her reverie and turn around. Larry's Range Rover had stopped in the middle of the road.

"What the fuck are you doing out here?" Larry's head appeared through the open car window.

"I've escaped from prison, and it's wonderful!" Ginny's grin was bigger than the scorching sun.

"Come back with me; you'll roast!" Larry opened the car door and began to walk towards her.

"I'm fine! Stop treating me like I'm a useless damsel in distress! I'll walk back in a minute!" She felt free; empowered, energised, and alive.

"Have you got your phone on you?" Irate and impotent, he stood his ground.

"It's in my pocket."

"Phone if you need me."

"Larry; please go home."

As the car moved away slowly she took one last look at the cows, who had registered no surprise whatsoever at the sudden interruption, and carried on chewing mesmerisingly. Smiling, she turned back towards the estate just as her phone vibrated. A flash of irritation seared into her good mood with the certain knowledge that the caller would either be Steve or Larry checking up on her. However, she was most surprised when Phil Desborough's number appeared on her screen.

"Hello Mr Desborough."

"It's Phil, remember?"

"Ah yes, Phil."

"Listen; I'm home now and have had a quick look at some of the photos on the computer. I recognise one of the men."

"Oh?" She stopped walking immediately as the investigator's words sunk in."

"Yeah; I've seen him before when I've had to give evidence in court. It's Judge Wittlingson."

"Oh Christ; it just gets better and better, doesn't it?" She sighed. "How on earth are we going to make the accusations stick?"

"We've got photographic evidence on our side. I'll hang around the offices and find out where they take the kids. Then we'll make plans from there."

"Thanks Phil."

"No problem."

She put the phone back in her pocket and walked back to the gate, deep in thought.

CHAPTER 17

"IT SEEMS STRANGE being in a supermarket again. I haven't bought any food for months and months." Ginny looked around at the bustling crowd of people hurrying to and fro with their metal trollies. "It's busier than I remember."

"All the kids have broken up from school don't forget." Larry pushed the trolley over to one side to let a mother pass with her four children. "Just get some extras for a barbeque tonight. We don't want to mess with the usual delivery."

"Perhaps we can invite Pat to eat with us before she goes off for a month. What do you say?" Ginny looked at Larry, who frowned.

"Nah; I'll have to watch my p's and q's. Won't even be able to fart in peace if I eat too much bread."

"It'd be a nice gesture." Ginny laughed, but did not hold out too much hope.

"What; farting?"

"No, you mong; inviting Pat for dinner."

"Leave it out. I'd rather invite Steve; at least you can have a laugh with him."

"Trudi will love these chicken kebabs. Chicken's the only thing I can get her to eat at the moment." Ginny put a packet of ten kebabs wrapped in cling film into the trolley. "I'll get some rice as well."

"What about some prawns?" Larry fished about in the freezer.

"Fine for you, but the midwife told me no seafood when she came last time."

"I know what." Larry turned towards her. "Shall we give an invite out to all the staff?" Perhaps have a pool party on Saturday night? I suppose it'll be a way of saying thanks for their work all year round, and we then won't have to entertain Pat on our own. Some of them will be going off soon for a week or two's holiday. What about it?"

"Sounds good." Ginny nodded. "I'll up the delivery on Friday. Shall we invite your sisters?"

"Nah; they're jealous and would only make snide remarks. Who needs that?"

As Larry drove the Range Rover drove back through the security gates, Ginny thought excitedly of plans for the pool party. On stepping out of the car and opening the main door, she checked out Steven, still sitting at the security desk.

"Tell your other guys we're having a pool party on Saturday night. You're all welcome. Let's say eight o'clock?" She looked questioningly at him.

"Sure thing. Thanks Mrs Ford." Steven gave a nod in her direction.

"Do call me Ginny; everyone else does, oh, except Pat." She laughed and rolled her eyes.

"Okay. Andy won't drink though, because he's on nights."

"That's fine; I'll get Bridget to make some of her iced lemonade."

When she heard Trudi's footsteps running down the stairs, Ginny stuck her head out of the kitchen door:

"Hey darling! Who's finished school for a month then?" She laughed and beckoned towards Pat Argent upstairs on the landing.

"Me! Miss Argent's only given me one essay to do. It's called 'What I did in the Summer Holidays', but I haven't done anything yet." Trudi made a face and opened the fridge.

"You'll be able to write about going to see Nanny and Grandad up in Yorkshire. We're going to stay with them for a week soon, before we fly to Malta for our holiday. You'll definitely be able to write about that." Ginny smiled at her daughter. "Daddy's going to get the barbeque out tonight, so you'll also be able to write about that."

"Yippee! Can I have burgers? You hardly ever let me eat burgers."

"What's a barbeque without burgers? I've been to the shops today to get you some. I've also got a few of those chicken kebabs you like."

"Yeah!" Trudi took a carton of orange juice from the fridge and danced about the room.

"I'm off now, Mrs Ford. I'll be back on the fourth of September." Pat Argent stood stiffly in the kitchen doorway, ill at ease and eager to go.

"We're having a pool party for the staff on Saturday night; you're very welcome to attend." Ginny ignored Larry making faces out in the hallway.

"Thank you for the invite, but I have other plans."

"I hope you have a good summer. There'll be a little bonus on your bank statement as a way of thanks." Ginny breathed a sigh of relief.

"Thank you. Trudi's work has improved no end. I look forward to returning in the autumn. When is the baby due, Mrs Ford?"

"At the end of January. We're very excited."

"Of course. I'll bid you farewell for now."

Trudi stood in the porch and waved at the Citroen's retreating bumper.

"Can I have a burger now, please?"

"Daddy's got to cook it first. Go find your cozzie, come out to the pool, and you can have a swim while you wait." Ginny felt a strange relief that the governess had left the house.

"Yeah!"

Larry had already lit the gas rings on the barbeque when Ginny reappeared in her bikini. She felt self-conscious of her slightly swollen abdomen, and wore a matching sarong.

"You look good enough to eat with these burgers." He kissed her and ran his hands down to her buttocks.

"Larry; stop it!"

"There's no cameras round the pool. Nobody can see anything."

"Trudi's on her way down. The last thing she wants to see is her parents necking like a couple of oversexed teenagers." She laughed. "Keep an eye on your burgers instead of me. Buggered burgers give you cancer anyway."

"Is that so? I'll attend to said burgers forthwith." He saluted and turned towards the barbeque.

"Mummy I can't find my cozzie!" Trudi wailed as she ran down the steps to the poolside area.

"Have a look in the changing room. There's probably a spare one in there." Ginny rearranged her sarong to cover her midriff, and made herself comfortable on a sun lounger.

"You'll have to jump in the pool in the rudie nudie if you can't find one!" Larry shouted as he added some sausages to the burgers and turned down the flame.

"Daddy! Don't be so gross!" Trudie's voice carried across the pool from the changing room.

Ginny chuckled as she idly gazed at the sun sparkling on the water; their little girl was growing up. The new baby's arrival would change the family dynamics about slightly, and Trudi might experience a bout of jealousy initially, but it was nothing that could not be coped with. Ginny knew her daughter would eventually adore her little brother or sister, and together they would grow to be a strong, powerful family unit.

CHAPTER 18

THE BEER WAS flowing a little too freely for Ginny's liking, and voices around her were becoming louder. She watched as Larry brought another barrel of ale out onto the patio, and hoped against hope that the drunken revelry would not awaken Trudi. With the exception of Andy, the rest of Steve's security guards and the team of gardeners were drinking like the proverbial fishes. Bridget and the largely female housekeeping staff had made polite conversation for the required ten minutes, and had long since disappeared.

"Great party Ginny; thanks a lot!" Steve's voice was slightly slurred as he downed yet another pint.

"Help yourself to the buffet." She nodded in the direction of a table groaning with chicken drumsticks, salad, jacket potatoes, coleslaw, French bread, and pasta, in the hope of Steve soaking up some of the excess alcohol.

"Cheers."

She watched him stagger slightly over towards the table. Larry, almost equally the worse for wear, also made his way to the food. The two men giggled at a private joke as they ate, making Ginny in her sober pregnant state feel rather left out. She was peckish, and decided to join them at the table.

"Hey Ginny!" Larry burped. "You're the love of my life!"

"You're drunk." Ginny helped herself to some chicken. "If you don't look out someone's going to fall into the pool and drown."

"Nah; we can take our beer." Steve slurred. "Hey Ginny – there's someone missing! Where's that private dick you hired? Wasn't he invited then?"

Ginny froze at Steve's words and gave him a stare. Genially vacant, he seemed oblivious to her facial expressions, and stuffed another piece of French bread into his mouth.

"There's a big secret. Naughty naughty. Where's the private dick?" He giggled like a young schoolboy.

"What private dick? What are you talking about?" Larry stopped eating and looked at Steve.

"Shhh!" Steve put a finger to his lips and giggled again. "It's a secret!"

Ginny walked away from them, hoping against hope that Larry was too far gone and would forget all about it. However, as she sat at the poolside with a plate of food she was dismayed to see her husband heading straight for her.

"Steve tells me you've hired a private investigator." He hiccupped and sat down heavily on a sun lounger.

"Larry, I don't think this is the right time to talk about it. " She looked around to ascertain how many people were within earshot.

"Well, that's where you're wrong!" Larry's words were becoming slurred and his rising tone sounded belligerent: "It's exactly the right time! I need to find out just how much danger you've put us in you stupid fucking woman!"

"I can't talk to you when you're drunk like this!" Her eyes filled with tears. "I'm going back inside! Leave me alone! Stay out here and drink yourself silly!" Putting her plate on the ground, she stood up tearfully and turned towards the steps.

"Everything alright down here?" Andy, sober as a judge, made his way down to the pool.

"Mind your own fucking business." Larry swayed slightly as he stood up to face the security guard.

"Ignore him Andy, it's the drink talking; he's pissed." Ginny pushed past Andy on the steps on her way to the house.

"I'm not pissed! I may be a lot of things, but pissed I'm not! Don't walk away from me!" He kicked the sun lounger out of the way, but then walked into the brick wall that was Andy Johnson.

Ginny could still see and hear the remonstrations as she reached the patio.

"Mrs Ford is crying. Let's calm down before we go back inside." Andy, six feet five inches in his socks, towered over Larry.

"You're not going anywhere, you fucker; you're fired!" Larry tried unsuccessfully to edge past Andy on the poolside.

"We'll see how things are in the morning. I've been paid for tonight's shift, and tonight's shift I will do."

"You're going now! Steve! Escort Andy out of the gate!" Larry looked around wildly for his new-found drinking buddy, who had collapsed onto one of the patio chairs.

"No; I'm going to sit here with you on this deckchair." Andy's voice was calm and in control of the situation.

Ginny wiped her eyes and looked down towards the pool. Andy had planted Larry firmly in a deckchair, and had pulled his own chair alongside. Andy looked up at her and signalled for a cup of coffee. She nodded to him and made her way to the kitchen. Switching on the kettle, she reached for the jar of coffee and added two heaped teaspoons into a mug. When the kettle boiled she stirred some milk into the hot, strong brew and took it outside.

"Your lovely wife has made you this." He took the mug from her. "Get it down the little red lane and then we can talk some more."

Ginny saw that Larry was suddenly as quiet as the proverbial lamb, as he drank from the mug.

"I love my wife." He started to sob as he looked at her and slurped. "I love everybody."

"That's super; now all we've got to do is get you up to bed." Andy winked at her as he took the empty cup from Larry's hands.

"I can do it myself, you arsehole." Larry reeled as he staggered to his feet.

"I thought you loved me, but now I'm an arsehole, eh?" Andy put an arm around Larry's back to steady him.

"Yeah; you're an arsehole."

"Think of me prowling the grounds keeping you safe tonight while you're tucked up in bed sleeping it off." Andy hauled Larry up the steps towards the patio."

"I don't care. You're still an arsehole. You're fired."

"Yeah, yeah. We'll talk about it in the morning."

CHAPTER 19

SHE FOLLOWED THE sound of snoring, and the stale smell of beer breath hit her as she popped her head around the door of the guest room. With Larry still sleeping it off, Ginny padded back to bed for a leisurely Sunday morning lie-in before Trudi skipped along for her usual snuggle.

However, she found that without Larry to cuddle up to she was wide awake and unable to doze. Reaching down on the floor beside the bed for her handbag, she fished about inside for her mobile phone, noticing that part of a message was displayed on the front screen. After tapping in her password, her mouth registered a small 'o' of surprise:

'I followed a well-dressed elderly lady last night in a dark blue BMW who came out of PhizzFace and drove four kids back to the Arlborough Boys' Home in Manor Way. I'll come round Monday lunchtime about 1pm to update, but I think I might have been spotted though. Phil.'

The text had been sent just after midnight. Ginny sat up in bed hugging her knees; head buzzing with thoughts running wildly around in her brain.

At last she had information about where the children were coming from! She also now knew that the abuse was definitely taking place on Friday evenings, and that Evelina still seemed to be carrying out her brothers' wishes.

Philip Desborough had excelled himself. Smiling, Ginny folded her arms on her knees and rested her chin on top, as the baby woke up and kicked about inside her.

Phizzface would be empty on Friday evenings; therefore the conference room would be an ideal place for paedophiles to meet. Security cameras could be switched off, and the Vecks would be free to do whatever they wanted.

The sound of Trudi's footsteps on the landing brought Ginny back to reality. Laying back on the pillows, she held out her arms as her daughter ran towards her.

"Where's Daddy?" Trudi looked about the bedroom and then bounced onto the bed.

"He had too much beer last night. He's sleeping in one of the guest bedrooms." Ginny kissed the top of her daughter's head and smoothed down her hair as the little girl snuggled into her arms.

"Ewwww. Will he be sick like last time?"

"I hope not, but Andy left him a bucket in there just in case."

"Yuck. Can I have some breakfast please?" Trudi wriggled out of Ginny's grasp and bounced up and down on the mattress.

"Okay; I can see you're not very tired anyway. Let's get up and Mummy will cook you some sausages and scrambled eggs." Ginny replaced the phone in her handbag and threw back the duvet.

"Marva cooks better than you."

"Oh she does, does she?"

"Why can't Marva cook my breakfast?"

"I've told you before; only the security staff work on Sundays, and Marva mostly comes in if we have lots of people staying over. You know she's not always here. We're seeing to ourselves today."

"I don't like your sausages; they taste funny."

"Well, have some cereal then. All you have to do is pour it out of the box; you can't go wrong."

"Okay."

Ginny liked Sundays; it was though the house belonged only to her and Larry again. With just the security staff changing shifts and keeping a low profile in the entrance hall, she felt freer and more in control. Descending the main staircase she wrapped her dressing gown around her more securely and waved to Andy monitoring the cameras.

"Morning Andy; you must be finishing soon?" She smiled at him and received an answering yawn.

"Excuse me; it's been a long night." He stretched his arms above his head. "Steve's still comatose on the deckchair. He'll be surfacing soon I expect though." Andy smiled. "Leon's at the gate. I'll let him in and then I'll be off."

"Thanks for getting Larry to bed. I owe you one."

"All in the line of duty." Andy yawned again.

Opening the kitchen door, she went to the fridge and took out a carton of milk, placing it on the long kitchen table next to her daughter.

"There you go; not even Mummy can spoil a bowl of cereal." She hid her hurt feelings and smiled. "I wonder if Marva can write books though?"

"Yes she can; she writes cookbooks." Trudi ate daintily from her spoon. "She told me. Can I watch a DVD when I've finished eating? She looked up hopefully.

"Yes, and when Daddy wakes up perhaps we'll go to the beach this afternoon."

From the kitchen window Ginny saw Steve stagger to his feet and look around bleary-eyed. She switched on the kettle and reached once more for the jar of coffee.

CHAPTER 20

"I WASN'T THAT far gone last night. What was Steve saying about a private dick?"

Larry stretched himself out full length on a towel, as Ginny sat up ramrod straight and kept her eyes focused on her daughter and a new-found friend as they shovelled sand into a castle-shaped plastic bucket amongst the crowds of sunburnt day-trippers and holidaymakers. Ginny's heart began to race.

"You sacked Andy last night. Do you remember that?" She glanced momentarily at him as she tried to alter the topic of conversation, noting his pale complexion and darker-than-usual sunglasses.

"No; why would I want to sack him? Don't talk wet." He sighed. "My mouth feels like the bottom of a parrot's cage."

"Whose fault is that?"

"Mine. Don't change the subject. Have you hired a private investigator?"

"Yes." She kept her eyes on the children so as not to see the expression on his face.

"For Pete's sake why? I can't believe you've done something like that without telling me." He sat up and stared at her.

"I had to do it. I couldn't live with myself anymore. Those poor kids are being abused, and we're living in the lap of luxury and doing sod all about it."

"I can live with being able to sit here freely on Arlborough beach and not having to look over my shoulder in case the Vecks have hired a hitman to shut us up." Larry *tutted* as he lay back down and put a sunhat over his face.

"Don't be so dramatic. Phil wouldn't give us away."

"Oh, so it's *Phil* now is it? How long have I been paying *Phil* for?" Larry lifted the sunhat and shot her a frozen glance.

"He hasn't been paid yet. He's coming to see me tomorrow and I'll give him a cheque then. He sent me a text this morning; he's found out where the kids are coming from. They're taken back afterwards to the Arlborough Boys' Home."

There was no reply from under the sunhat. Ginny smiled at Trudi, who waved a small red spade at her. The sound of the waves and the seagulls bridged the deafening silence between them.

"I've got to have you on my side in this, Larry. Just imagine if it was Trudi being taken there and abused. Wouldn't you want somebody to try and do something about it?" Ginny turned towards him, pleading and on the verge of tears.

Larry exhaled audibly as he sat up.

"Yes of course I would. It's just that the more people who know, then the more our world is going to be turned upside down. I'm going to have to employ more security staff; it has a knock-on effect. Until the Vecks are taken down then we'll be prisoners inside the estate. It won't be easy; they've been paying people off all their lives. We fell for it; so will others."

"We didn't have a choice as I remember. They had Trudi."

"But now they haven't! They probably know where we are, but they've left us alone and we ought to do the same for them."

"I can't, Larry. That poor child's face tied up on the chair did it for me."

"We're going to be looking over our shoulders for the rest of our lives." He dropped his head down towards his knees. "Is that what you want?" He sighed and shook his head.

"What I want and what I must do are two different things; someone somewhere in authority will refuse to be paid off by these people. We've got to find out who that somebody is." She put her hand on his back and caressed his bare warm skin.

"And until we find that person we'll be in danger." Larry was unresponsive to her touch.

"They can't trace Phil back to us."

"Let's hope not, but they've got too much to lose to be lax with security. Think about it; they probably employ guys to protect Evelina and the kids."

Ginny thought back to the text she had received that morning.

"There's something else I've got to tell you about."

"Jeez; what now?" He sat up straight and looked at her.

"Phil thought he was followed last night."

"Ginny; what have you done? They've probably already checked out his number plate and found out who he is through the police!" Larry rolled his eyes heavenwards. "You've bolloxed up everything… the good life we've had this past year…… everything!" He flopped back down on the towel and closed his eyes.

Ginny's eyes filled with tears, as all around her happy families picnicked on the sand.

"I'm sorry but I can't help it. I want to help that little boy. His face haunts my every waking moment. Please don't go against me; I couldn't bear it if you hate me."

Larry reached out, sighed again, and took her hand in his.

"I don't hate you; I love you. In a way I admire you for wanting to do something for the kid. It's just that I've a sneaky feeling we now haven't heard the last of the Vecks."

"Phil was careful I'm sure. He's coming to the house tomorrow. We can speak to him then."

"Let's get Trudi home now though; just in case."

As they gathered up their belongings, Ginny felt relieved on getting everything out in the open, but could not help a growing sinking feeling in the pit of her stomach.

CHAPTER 21

"SO WHERE'S DICK then?" Larry checked his watch.

"His name's Phil, I told you. He'll be here in a minute." Ginny uncovered some plates of pre-prepared finger food.

"I'm starving; he'll have to eat his when he gets here." Larry chomped on a tuna and sweetcorn sandwich.

"I don't like tuna." Trudi wrinkled her nose and began to peer at the fillings inside the bread

"Don't touch the food if you're not going to eat it." Ginny sent a frown in her daughter's direction.

"What else is there then?"

Trudi's whining tone began to irritate Ginny, who was already on edge. She looked at the clock again.

"There's some prawn and mayonnaise wraps there; take one of those."

"Yummy. When's Tom coming to play?"

"At the weekend."

"I don't want to wait that long, can I ask Rachel?"

"Yes, but after we've spoken to Mr Desborough."

"I don't think he's coming." Larry took another sandwich.

"I'll phone him; I've got his number."

Ginny took her iPhone from her handbag and found the contact details.

"There's a continuous sound like it's been disconnected." She frowned again as she took the phone away from her ear and looked at the screen.

"Try again." Larry took a handful of crisps.

"Can I have some crisps, Daddy?" Trudi looked hopefully towards her father.

"What's the magic word?" Larry held the container of crisps high in the air.

"Per…lea….se!"

"Okay; leave some for Mummy though."

Ginny carefully redialled.

"It's no good; it's not ringing." She stood up. "I'll put a couple of sandwiches in the fridge for him and a piece of cake." She took a clean plate from the pile. "He definitely said he'd be here about one o'clock though."

"It's a quarter to two now." Larry shrugged. "We'll have to hang around here and wait for him."

"Can I go swimming after lunch?" Trudi reached over and took a second wrap.

"Not straight away. Tell you what; if you write a bit of your essay for Miss Argent while we talk to the man who is coming to see us, then when he's gone Daddy will get in the pool with you. How's that?" Larry smiled as he ate.

"Writing's boring, but………oh, okay then." Trudi kicked her feet against the chair. "Is that a promise, Daddy?"

"Cross my heart." Larry nodded.

Ginny's sinking feeling of doom and gloom persisted as the afternoon sun sank lower in the sky with still no sign of Phil Desborough, and with repeated unsuccessful attempts to contact him by phone. She sat by the pool and watched as her husband and daughter splashed about happily, unable to shake off the certainty that something was dreadfully wrong. After preparing a buffet salad for dinner and bringing it out onto the patio, Ginny found that she could only pick at a piece of chicken and move some rice about on her plate with a fork.

"Come on love; try to eat. Our baby needs some nourishment." Larry smiled and ruffled her hair.

"It's no good; until I know what's happened to Phil I can't settle to anything." She put her plate down on the floor and lay back on the sun lounger with a sigh.

"Do you know where he lives?" Larry kept one eye on his daughter, as Trudi helped herself to a chicken drumstick and some salad.

"No; only that he has a house not too far away in the centre of Arlborough. Leon would know; Phil's his brother in law."

"That's the answer then." Larry waved his fork about in the air. "When Leon starts work tonight I'll ask him to phone his sister and find out what's going on."

"I expect he's been held up. He'll be here tomorrow; he's not going to turn down the chance of being paid, is he?"

Ginny picked up her plate again, finding she was suddenly hungry.

As the evening shadows lengthened and day turned into night, Ginny came back downstairs after reading Trudi a bedtime story, and was surprised to see Andy sitting at the security desk.

"Where's Leon? I thought he was on duty tonight?" She smiled and tried to hide her disappointment.

Andy looked up briefly from monitoring the screens.

"Hi; there's been some sort of family crisis. Leon's brother-in-law is missing; nobody's seen him since Saturday evening. Leon's helping with the search. Haven't you seen the TV today? It'll be on the local news tonight for sure."

Ginny ran through to the main lounge and switched on the television. She signalled to Larry through the open patio door, her heart beating wildly. When he joined her she almost fell into his arms.

"Phil Desborough's gone missing! Leon's out helping to search for him. Andy says there's something on the local news about it!"

She pulled out of his embrace and began to pace about the room, impatient for information.

"Come and sit down, love. It's no use getting worked up until we know the facts."

She could take no comfort from his usual steadfast manner in a crisis. Steeling herself for the worst, she sat down next to him on the sofa.

In our local news tonight, a car is pulled out of the Arlborough River. A body inside the car had one ear missing, and has been identified as private investigator Philip Desborough, who had not been seen since Saturday evening. Police have begun their enquiries, and anybody with any knowledge should contact the helpline number which will be given out at the end of the programme.'

Ginny's blood ran cold. She was aware that Larry had fallen silent.

"It's no use going to the police; they'll do nothing." She fought a rising panic. "With one ear missing, he'd obviously been tortured. If he told them who he was working for, we're stuffed."

Larry stood up, his brow furrowed.

"We'll close the house down early for a couple of weeks and leave for your parents' place tomorrow. It's only a little bit sooner, but they'll be pleased to be able to make a longer fuss of Trudi. From there we'll catch the plane as planned from Manchester to Luqa airport. We'll get away and think about what to do when we get to Malta."

When she went to the fridge for some milk to make a mug of tea, Philip Desborough's tuna sandwiches and slice of fruit cake still lay on the top shelf where she had placed them. Tearfully she tore off the cling film wrap and put them in the bin.

CHAPTER 22

A WALL OF heat hit them as they stepped out of the plane at Luqa airport. Ginny, holding Trudi's hand, walked down the steps onto the tarmac.

"I'm glad we're in a hotel with a lot of other people around. It'll be good for Trudi too."

Larry followed behind her on the way to the main airport building.

"We'll have a nice break, but I have to be back by the middle of next week to oversee the opening of the club."

"Can't it wait? I don't want you to leave the estate when we get home."

"I've been thinking; we can't put our lives on hold forever. The Vecks might not have a clue who Desborough was working for."

"If they found the memory stick I gave him or he told them about us, then they *will* know."

"I need the toilet, Mummy."

"Okay. We'll find the ladies' room while Daddy hires a car." Ginny waved to Larry as he walked towards the car rental kiosk.

"Where will we drive to?" Trudi skipped along beside her.

"The Seabank hotel in Mellieha. We've rented a family suite on the top floor. The hotel's right across the road from the beach."

"Goody; can I have a ride on a jet ski?"

"Only if Daddy's with you."

As she walked back into the main airport building with Trudi, she could see that Larry had reached the front of the queue. He turned to smile at her.

"We've got an Audi, with satnav and air-conditioning."

"I can't wait to sit in it." Ginny wiped the sweat from her brow.

"The chap says it's about twenty three kilometres to Mellieha; maybe half an hour's drive. Even better; they drive on the left."

"Brilliant! This holiday is just what we needed." Ginny swung Trudi's hand to and fro, and felt somewhat lighter in mood.

After Larry's slalom-type driving trying to avoid many of the island's potholes, Ginny was feeling slightly nauseous and was rather relieved when he swung the Audi into the hotel car park. She craned her neck out of the car window, and caught a glimpse of Mellieha bay curving around a deep blue sea frilled with frothy waves whipped up by the wind.

"I can see jet skis and paddle boats!" Trudi undid her seat belt and kneeled up on the back seat to get a better view.

"You can have a go with Daddy tomorrow, but first we need to find our suite and unpack."

"Aw….boring!"

"Mummy feels sick; the roads were a bit bumpy." Ginny opened the car door, glad to get out.

"Let's find our room. You can have a lie down, and Trudi and me will go and have a look around." Larry lifted the luggage out of the boot. "I'm not pulling along a pink suitcase with a big picture of a Barbie doll on the front. This one's all yours, Trude." He wheeled the case over in Trudi's direction.

"Daddy, you're horrible." Trudi grasped the handle of the suitcase. "Is there a games room and a swimming pool?"

"Yep; so it said in the brochure."

Ginny was glad that somebody had left the air-conditioning on low when they reached the family suite. The king-size bed looked inviting, and she sunk down gratefully onto the crisp counterpane.

"Sorry; I just need to have a doze. I'm hot, tired, and feel icky." She closed her eyes, needing to shut out the world while the baby was quiet inside her; seemingly asleep after the rocking and rolling of the car journey.

"Don't worry; I'll grab our swimming things and some towels from the cases and take Trude out to the pool."

The noise of the seagulls and the traffic outside was muted by double glazing. Ginny remembered nothing more until she awoke about an hour later, feeling confused by the new surroundings, but relatively refreshed and rather hungry.

After a quick shower she unpacked the cases and tried on her new maternity swimsuit, wrinkling her nose at the reflection of her hardened protruding abdomen in the mirror. Wrapping a matching sarong around her middle, she put on some flip-flops, caught the lift down to the ground floor, and made her way out through the foyer to the back of the hotel. She waved at Larry, sitting on the edge of the pool and kicking his heels against the tiles.

"Hey! Feeling better now, love?" He stood up to greet her.

"Much, thanks. I see Trudi's found a friend already." She waved at her daughter, splashing about in the shallow end with another girl about the same age.

"Yeah; I'm redundant now. I'm just playing lifeguard." He chuckled and indicated towards three sunbeds under straw umbrellas. "I've grabbed those beds for us. We can keep an eye on her from there."

He stood up, but still kept his eyes on the shallow end of the pool.

"I had a look at the noticeboard and there's a meeting with the rep tonight after dinner. We'll be able to ask where the local touristy spots are."

Ginny stretched out on the sunbed.

"I know Trudi will like the Popeye village where they made the film. I read about it on the Internet. There's also boat trips from Valetta to the Blue Lagoon." She poked her tongue out at him. "See; I've done my homework already."

"You should have been a rep." Larry altered the back of the sunbed so that he could sit up straight.

"Nah; wouldn't want old men in their Speedos thinking they're God's gift and making passes at me."

"Sounds good fun actually. Perhaps I'll have a go with the rep tonight. Did you pack my Speedos?"

"Thankfully, no."

CHAPTER 23

"SHE'S ASLEEP; WORN out I think. It's been a long day. Funny to think that only this morning we were in England." Ginny stepped out onto the balcony and smiled at Larry hanging out the wet swimming costumes and towels. "You old washerwoman, you."

"A woman's work is never done. Just look at my washday hands!" Larry inspected his palms and chuckled.

"Have you had any thoughts on what we're going to do when we get home?" Ginny took two plastic chairs off a stack at one end of the balcony, and placed them side by side. She sat down and motioned for Larry to do the same.

"I've been thinking. If we can't contact the police, then we'll have to get in touch with the NSPCC; I'll look them up on Google and find out if there's a helpline. Also when a mate of mine thought he'd been treated unfairly by the police a few years back, he contacted some organisation that investigates them." Larry flopped down in the chair and looked out to sea.

"What's that?" Ginny turned towards him as she sat down.

"I think it's called 'Police Complaints' or something similar. I'll have to call him and ask. I just know they investigate if there's any question of police integrity. All is not lost, love; the NSPCC will hopefully get in touch with the children's services who can investigate and get the kids taken away from that home, and the other people can check up on our bent police chief when I find out who they are. We've still got another copy of the memory stick in the safe as evidence. As long as we've got that we're laughing. I'm going to phone Steve and tell him to step up security on the estate."

Ginny sighed, looked down, and found she was wringing her hands.

"It's all my fault. You were right; I've opened up a whole can of worms, and now somebody has been murdered because of me. I killed Philip Desborough; God, what have I done?" She put her hands over her face and shook her head.

"No, the Vecks had him killed. You did what you thought was right. It was noble of you to try and do something to save the kids. We've got to see it through now. Somebody's been murdered, and we can't let them get away with it. I think we ought to phone the NSPCC and also find out a bit more about the police complaints' thing while we're out here in Malta. In that way the Vecks can be arrested and hopefully charged while we're miles away. What do you think?"

Ginny nodded.

"It's a good idea. Let's do it now; I can't think of anything better. I'll nip down to Reception and get the password for the Internet connection."

"You sit there. I'll go. I'll be back in a minute."

From her vantage point on the balcony Ginny, deep in thought, looked down at the happy carefree couples strolling hand-in-hand along the beachfront promenade. *The consequences of the one phone call she should never have made had been far reaching.*

Were they now in mortal danger?

With the outcome of her actions weighing heavily on her mind, she stood up and walked through to the small single bedroom, where Trudy slept in a tangle of arms, legs, and bedclothes. She kissed her child's forehead, rearranged the covers, and then walked to the entrance door of the suite on hearing a light tapping. Looking through the security peephole she could see Larry's face staring back at her, distorted through the lens.

"I forgot my key. I've got the password." Larry waved a small piece of paper in the air.

"Let's get online now. I just want it all over with." She closed the door behind him.

She moved Trudi's crayons and colouring book out of the way, placed their iPad on the table, and logged in.

"Here's the NSPCC site. Ah….they have a twenty four hour helpline, and we can remain anonymous; look…" She moved slightly to one side to let Larry have a better view.

"There's a form we can fill in if we don't want to call." Larry scrolled down the page.

"I'd rather speak to somebody; in that way they'll be able to act on it straight away."

"Okay. Do you want to call, or shall I?"

Ginny knew the answer to Larry's question without even thinking about it.

"It's my mess; I got us into this. I'll make the call. I saw instructions somewhere on how to make international calls." She looked around the room. "I think I put it on top of the TV."

"Yeah, here it is." Larry reached over and grabbed a laminated A4 size sheet of paper and glanced through it quickly. "It's a doddle. Just dial a nine for an outside line, and then two zeros, two fours, the area code, and then the number."

"Hello; this is the NSPCC Helpline; how can I help?"

The reassuring female voice on the other end of the phone line quietened Ginny's racing heart somewhat.

"Hello. I'm on holiday in Malta, but I'm phoning about some children I am concerned about, who live in Arlborough Boys' Home in the UK."

"Thank you for making this call. I'm Sandra. This conversation will be recorded, but I can reassure you that any details you give about yourself or the children concerned will remain confidential. The NSPCC will never disclose your name or contact details, but you can choose to remain anonymous if you prefer. We will act immediately upon any information you give us."

Ginny took a deep breath.

"My name is Mrs Virginia Ford. I live in Meadowleas Manor, which is on the Vinery Road about 10 miles from the centre of Arlborough. I have photographic evidence on a memory stick of child abuse taking place in the conference room of PhizzFace Incorporated, twenty eight to thirty five

High Street, Arlborough. The perpetrators of this crime are all people in authority; Randolph, Dennis and Evelina Veck, who are the three main directors of PhizzFace. There's also incriminating photos of the chief inspector of police for the Arlborough division, I think his surname is Greensmith. Also present in the photos are Judge Wirtlingson, and lastly Mike Farnes of the Arlborough Standard newspaper. I don't know if any other people are involved. I hired a private detective to find out where the boys came from. He was followed by somebody probably working for the Vecks, and has since been murdered. However, he found out before his death that all the children live in the Arlborough Boys' Home. Please can you help us? I'm not sure if any of the staff at the home are involved too."

The words came out in a rush, but the relief on Ginny's face was almost palpable.

"Thank you for calling. We shall act straight away and make an urgent referral to Social Services. As the integrity of the police is also an issue here, we will be contacting the IPCC, the Independent Police Complaints' Commission, instead of going directly through to the Arlborough Police Department. I'll go through your story again with you in a minute, just to make sure I've got all the correct details, and if you'd like to leave me a contact number I will update you on the case as soon as there is some news. As I said before, your contact details will remain confidential."

"Thank you." Ginny's heart slowed to a normal rhythm. "The memory stick is in our safe at home. The Christian names of the boys are on the photos. One boy called Zac is particularly affected. We will be back in the UK by next Sunday evening, and can make a copy of the memory stick's contents to give to whoever needs it."

"Thank you Mrs Ford; you have done the right thing in contacting us. Somebody from the IPCC will be in contact for the memory stick. Are you happy for us to proceed?"

"Yes; oh, yes."

When at length she ended the call, she fell into Larry's welcome arms and sobbed like a baby.

CHAPTER 24

"I'M SO PLEASED I phoned them."

Ginny, holding Trudi's hand, queued up along the gangplank of the Seahawk at Valletta harbour.

"Hopefully they'll be arrested soon, and then perhaps when they've got the evidence from us they can charge them." Larry, standing behind, kissed the back of her neck.

"Last night was the best night's sleep I've had in ages. I'm really looking forward to today's trip. The Blue Lagoon sounds beautiful!" She turned and smiled at him.

"*You're* beautiful. I'm so sorry I gave you such a hard time." Larry kissed her.

"Don't worry. I still feel guilty though about Phil Desborough."

"There's nothing more we can do now." Larry shrugged his shoulders as he moved forward in the queue.

The Seahawk slowly filled up with tourists. Ginny and Larry found a seat at the front of the boat, as Trudi kneeled between them and looked over the rail.

"Can we jump off the boat and swim in the sea today, like the rep said?" Trudi leaned over further.

"Yes, the boat will stop at lunchtime for a brief swim, and then you'll be able to have another dip in the lagoon a bit later on." Ginny put an arm firmly around one of her daughter's legs. "I've brought some snorkels as well for you and Daddy; apparently the water is so clear and blue there that you can see all the fish swimming about in it."

"I can't wait!"

"You must stay with Daddy though. No swimming off on your own. The rep said the current is strong there."

"Aren't you coming in the water, Mummy?"

"I will at lunchtime, but I might just sit and watch later on."

As the boat pulled away from the pier, Ginny closed her eyes and relished the cooling breeze on her face. The chatter of the passengers faded into the background, as she leaned back against the seat and felt the thrum of the engines. After half an hour or so she sensed Trudi becoming restless.

"I'll take her up on the top deck for a while. Are you coming up?" Larry took hold of Trudi's hand and stood up.

"Why not? I'll get some drinks from the bar."

Ginny climbed a steep staircase up to the top deck with some cold bottles of fruit juice. Several passengers were already changing into swimming gear in preparation for the lunchtime stop.

"There's a diving board up there; see? I'm going to dive off that at lunchtime." Larry grinned and pointed to the top of the boat.

"Is that wise?"

"Nothing I haven't done at Arlborough public baths before they took the high diving boards away for our 'safety'." Larry held up two index fingers and wiggled them to emphasise the last word.

"Probably because some teenage boy had nearly killed himself diving off the topmost board." Ginny sipped her drink and looked upwards. "Why do you have to do something so dangerous?"

"Because I'm a bloke and because it's there." He grinned at her again.

"I'm going to jump off that board, because I can't dive yet." Trudi wrapped a towel around her and began to change into a swimsuit.

"You'll do no such thing. You can swim near the boat with Mummy." Ginny shook her head.

"Boring!"

"Boring or not, that's what you'll be doing."

When the engines ceased throbbing and the anchor was dropped, the boat floated serenely on the sea. A queue started to build up behind the diving board.

"I'm going to have a couple of dives and then we can have our lunch." Larry took off his shorts to reveal his swimming trunks underneath. "If you and Trudi swim around near the ladder, I'll come round and find you."

The water was warm, although somehow cooling at the same time. Ginny climbed down the ladder and reached out her arms towards Trudi.

"I can swim on my own!" Trudi flipped over on her back and floated.

"Come around the side of the boat and you can see Daddy dive."

Ginny, with Trudi close by, floated on the waves as Larry launched himself headfirst horizontally off the rooftop board, executing a perfect, almost poetical dive into the water. Surfacing near the boat, he grinned and rubbed the salt from his eyes.

"That was awesome! One more and then I'm going to have something to eat."

Her eyes watched as his muscular thighs climbed the ladder back up to the roof. She loved the bones of him. Their baby woke up and floated about in her womb as she swirled around in the sea. She wanted to clasp him and Trudi to her breast and never let them go.

CHAPTER 25

"IT'S STEVE, GINNY. Is Larry there?"

Ginny looked across to where Larry, slouching in a deckchair, faced the evening sun and rested his feet on the rail of their balcony.

"It's Steve." She handed him the phone.

"Hey Steve." He yawned. "This holiday malarkey is hard work."

Ginny relaxed and closed her eyes, lulled by the sound of the waves. However, after a few moments had passed she was aware that Larry was not making any sound at all. Puzzled and suddenly alert, she opened her eyes again and wriggled upright. Her husband's face was unusually pale as he sat hunched forward with his mouth open and the phone pressed to his ear.

"What's up?" She hissed at him.

Impatient after receiving a dismissive wave, she tried to piece together both sides of the conversation while searching his features for clues at the same time. Eventually, full of foreboding, she sat back in the deckchair and waited until he had ended the call.

"Fuck; somebody's got into the house while we've been away." He flopped back and exhaled noisily.

"Who? What's been taken?" She felt a rising panic flood through her body.

"Steve's not sure. Bridget and her girls have tidied up, but he says the safe's been forced."

"Oh shit; the memory stick! The Vecks must have been arrested and sent somebody to find it. I thought you'd increased security?" She reached over and grabbed his hand.

"I hadn't got round to phoning Steve. Andy was on his own and got done over last night while he was outside. He's doing okay now, but was jumped from behind and doesn't know who knocked him out. I wish we'd taken the bloody phones out on that boat today. You heard; I've told Steve to call Sean in with the dogs. We've got to go back." He disengaged her hand, stood up, and put his elbows on the balcony rail. "This is a fucking nightmare."

Further guilt washed over her.

"Oh God; this is all my fault. I've done the most stupid thing!"

"No; this is personal now. Leon's lost his brother-in-law; Andy's been beaten up. I'm going to nail those Vecks if it's the last thing I do on this earth." His hands unknowingly bunched into fists. "Where's the iPad? I'll see if there's a flight back in the morning."

"I'll get it. Trudi will be so disappointed though." She sighed and stood up. "What else was in the safe?"

"A few thousand pounds to pay the wages, plus the memory stick. I should have buried it like I did in the old house. Thank Christ we keep valuables in the bank."

"What if someone else gets in?" She shuddered. "We could be murdered in our beds!"

"They've got what they wanted. The dogs will roam outside at night with Sean. We'll be perfectly safe." She thought he might be sounding more confident than he felt. "I'll double the security in the house until the Vecks are put away."

"There's no evidence now; they'll get off." She looked at him. "It's their word against ours."

Following behind as Larry went back into the suite, Ginny was aware that an invisible dark cloud had descended upon them. Silently she watched as Larry checked the flights.

"Here's one; it leaves at two o'clock tomorrow afternoon. Plenty of time to get back to the airport. We'll go away again in the autumn. Everything might have blown over by then."

"Who's going to tell Trudi? She was looking forward to going to the Popeye village."

"That's the least of our worries now."

She clung to the safety of Larry's body in the darkness of the unfamiliar bed. Confirmation that a malicious stranger had violated their home was causing a myriad of unwelcome thoughts to buzz around inside her head.

"Shall we send Trudi to Mum and Dad's for a couple more weeks? She'll be safe there until we know what's happening about the Vecks."

"Sure; you need to stay there as well." Larry squeezed her shoulder.

"No; I'm probably going to be needed to testify I expect."

"If only we had another memory stick." Larry's sigh was audible over the hum of the air-conditioning.

"How about asking Leon's sister if she knows anything, like whether Phil might have hidden it somewhere?"

"She'll still be grieving; I wouldn't want to bother her now."

"If he told her everything she might want to nail the Vecks as much as we do."

He turned on his side and wrapped both arms around her.

"Give us a kiss before it all goes tits up tomorrow."

"It's already gone tits up." She lifted her head and touched his lips with her own.

"Love you, Ginny. We'll get through this; it'll be okay."

"Love you too; I'm so sorry about everything." She buried her face in his chest.

"Together we're strong. Now go to sleep; don't worry." He kissed the top of her head.

She wanted to stay in the cocoon of his warmth forever.

CHAPTER 26

THE RAIN DROVE sideways through the open window of the Range Rover.

"Steve; we're back." Larry spoke through the intercom as the gates unlocked.

Ginny looked over her shoulder at the empty back seat.

"It seems so strange without Trudi."

"It's for the best. Your dad was a trooper, driving all that way to pick her up from the airport. I want her miles away from here at the moment." Larry drove slowly up the driveway as the gates closed behind them.

"Any problems overnight?" Larry stepped out of the car and acknowledged Steve walking towards him.

"All quiet. Is anybody going to tell me what the hell is going on?" Steve shrugged his shoulders.

"Let's go into the study; I'm getting wet. Sorry mate; I should have told you a while back."

Ginny looked around her fearfully as they stood in the rain on the driveway.

"Where else in the house was disturbed?" She looked at Steve. "I feel like somebody's watching me."

"Various drawers and cupboards were turned out as though they were looking for something. There's nobody here now except us and Rick, who's covering for Andy. Sean will come in about six o'clock with the dogs." Steve began to walk towards the house.

"Was our newspaper delivered today?" Ginny had to walk quickly to keep up with Steve's long strides.

"Yeah, along with the post. It's all in the study on the desk. Where's Trudi?"

"Back with her nanny and grandad many miles from here. Poor Trude; one minute she was on holiday and the next minute she was being whisked away to my parents. I'm never going to hear the last of it when she gets home."

"It's for the best."

"That's what I said." Larry turned the handle of the study door. "Bridget's done a fine job in tidying up."

"Yeah; the girls were at it for two days."

"There'll be a bonus for them."

Ginny gasped when she saw the door of the safe swinging on its hinges.

"They must have employed a safecracker for this job."

"Nothing's beyond them." Larry checked inside the safe. "Empty, but then I never expected otherwise."

"*Who* must have employed a safecracker? Steve stood squarely in the doorway, arms folded. "If I'm to do my job properly I need to know what I'm up against."

Larry sat down with a sigh in his office chair. Ginny perched herself on the desk and listened.

"Ginny once found a memory stick that incriminates the Veck brothers; the main directors of PhizzFace, along with members of the police and several others. You know; they've got their headquarters in Arlborough High Street."

"My wife buys their night cream; it costs me a bloody fortune." Steve smiled wryly.

"Yeah; well, the fuckers are paedophiles."

"Christ."

"Leon's brother-in-law found out where they were getting the kids from. As you know he was tortured before he was found; it's obvious to Ginny and me that they were trying to find out if he had a copy of the memory stick."

"Did he?"

"Yeah; we made him a copy to see if he could recognise any of the bastards. He said one of them was Judge Wittlingson." Larry paused as Steve whistled softly under his breath. "We don't know if Phil gave it up to them or not when he was tortured."

"I'll ask Lena if she knows anything. We're friends of the family."

"Cheers Steve; that'll be a great help." Ginny nodded. "We reported them to the authorities while we were away; was there anything in the papers about it?"

"Not really, given the seriousness of it. I remember something on the local news though, but as I didn't know anything I didn't associate it with you. Anyway, the kids were playing up, and I never got to hear it all."

"That figures; one of them is the editor of the Arlborough Standard. There may be others from the newspaper implicated who don't want it broadcast. It's an ever-widening circle." She jumped down from the desk to pace about the room. "I'm afraid this break-in may only be the start. We're part of the backlash from the arrests, I expect. They wanted to make sure no evidence exists before they go to trial."

"When I finish my shift I'll go and see Lena. Phil must have said *something* to her about it."

"How's she doing?" Ginny's guilt resurfaced. "Did they have any children?"

"No kids thankfully; they hadn't been married that long. She's coping; she's staying with Leon and Val at the moment."

"Thanks Steve. We're going to unpack now; I'll leave you to carry on."

"Sure thing Ginny. With the extra security I'm sure we'll be fine."

She remained on edge until after dinner, when the sight of Bridget's son Sean accompanied by three huge German shepherd dogs on leads eased her mind somewhat. She waved to him from the front door, but warily kept her distance.

"Hi Sean; are you okay working here at night for the next few weeks?"

"That's fine Mrs Ford. I'll go when Mum starts work in the mornings; she nags me to find a girlfriend, and she doesn't like the dogs."

"I don't blame her; I'm not going a bundle on them myself." Ginny smiled and looked away from one dog giving her the evil eye.

"Ah; to be sure they're little sweethearts." Sean patted their heads. "They'll only kill if I tell them to."

"How reassuring. All the same, I don't think I'll be going out for a midnight walk."

"As you wish, Mrs Ford. As you wish."

Ginny closed the door and gave a huge sigh of relief.

CHAPTER 27

"GINNY, STEVE'S HAD some news."

She looked up from the sun lounger as Larry came towards her, grinning. Her heart immediately started pounding, waking the baby and making it kick.

"What?"

"Have you opened the post since we came back from Malta?"

"No; I left it for you like I always do." She looked at him quizzically.

"I've only just got round to picking it up. Look!" He waved a piece of card under her nose.

"What's that?" She tried to peer closer to get a better view.

"Steve just told me that he went to see Lena yesterday. She said Phil was edgy before he went out on that last day, and gave her a parcel to post. He said for her to hide it, but to put it in the post if something happened to him. She posted it here, Ginny!"

"We haven't received any parcels." She shook her head.

"No; we've been away. This is a card to say there's something at the sorting office. She posted it by registered mail. We've got to sign for it; I bet it's Phil's parcel!" He bent down and kissed her smack on the lips.

"It's Phil's memory stick!" Ginny leapt from the sunbed and flung her arms around Larry. "We've got our evidence back!"

"It's got to be! Let's go there now and pick it up!" Larry swung her around "Blimey, you're getting heavy!"

"Blame junior; it's all your fault." She laughed and kissed him. "Poor Phil; if he had given them what they wanted he might still be alive."

"We'll get the bastards yet; come on, let's go!"

Quickly throwing on a sundress over her bikini, Ginny looked over her shoulder at Steve as she followed Larry out through the front door.

"We're going to pick up Phil's parcel from the sorting office." She smiled at him.

"Okay." Steve kept one eye on the monitors. "See you later."

Waving her left hand, Ginny acknowledged a black Mondeo giving way for their Range Rover to turn right out of the main gates. A shimmering afternoon heat had descended, and she smiled when the driver passed an arm through the open sunroof and waved back. With many people away on summer holidays and the schools closed, the winding country road was unusually traffic-free. Larry reached the centre of town in only 15 minutes, and backed into a shady spot just off the main thoroughfare. As the reversing sensors bleeped, Ginny searched in her bag for some ID. After climbing out of the Range Rover she slipped her hand in his as they waited for a car to pass by in order to be able to cross the road into the sorting office.

"He's in no hurry, is he?" Larry stood impatiently on the pavement.

"Isn't that driver who waved to us when we left home?" Ginny's eyes followed the Mondeo as it drove past.

"Yeah; I think so. He was behind us all the way into town."

There were only a few people ahead of them in the queue. The sorting office was pleasantly air-conditioned, and they enjoyed a brief time to cool off. After showing her ID at the counter, Ginny signed with an electronic pen and took possession of a small parcel showing an Arlborough postmark, wrapped in brown paper:

"Open it up, Gin; let's see what's in it." Larry looked the parcel up and down.

"I will, when we get back to the car." Ginny decided to take no chances with security.

The horse chestnut's branches had kept the Range Rover tolerably cool. Ginny climbed up into the front seat and tore open the parcel. Inside, wrapped in a carelessly torn-off piece of paper, was Phil Desborough's copy of the memory stick.

"We're back in the race!" Larry whistled and banged the steering wheel with both fists.

"There's a note." Ginny sighed with relief as she unfolded a single sheet of paper.

"What does it say?" Larry craned his neck to see.

Dear Mrs Ford, I think I may have been followed back to my home this evening. I tracked an old lady, a security guy and four youngsters. One was about ten years old, and the others younger. They were all taken back to the Arlborough Boys' Home. I'm sending this in the post to you just in case for any reason I don't make the meeting on Monday. Phil'

"Poor sod; he knew something was up." Larry shook his head. "Give it to me; I'm going to bury it in the grounds until it's needed for evidence." He slid the memory stick into the top pocket of his shirt, buttoned it down, and started the engine.

"Let's go home. I need a dip in the pool; I'm melting." Ginny looked down and patted her abdomen. "Soon I'm going to have to just use the lap belt."

"Aren't pregnant women exempt?"

"No; I'll have to use the one that goes under the bump instead."

The car picked up speed as it headed towards the junction with the main road. The last thing she remembered before her head hit the side window was Larry shouting out something about spongy brakes.

CHAPTER 28

WHY WERE THE reversing sensors still bleeping? Ginny opened her eyes and tried to concentrate on somebody's hazy features looking down upon her.

"Ginny! Thank God!"

It was Larry's voice, but his face kept going in and out of focus. The bleeping noise began to accelerate as she struggled to sit up.

"You're in hospital. Stay laying down, Gin. I got away with whiplash, but you've had concussion. The car's brake lines were cut; I bet it was something to do with the guy in the Mondeo. Some old boy crashed into the side of us near the sorting office yesterday."

She struggled to take in the news. Nausea washed over her, and her head throbbed with pain. She felt something bulky between her legs. Larry's fingers entwined around hers. She felt the warmth of his hand.

"Thank God for the Range Rover. Any other car and we could have died."

Died.

Yesterday?

She could have died!

The baby could have died!

The baby!

Something bulky between her legs!

"No……..!" Ignoring the waves of sickness she reached down under the blanket.

"Ginny; you've lost the baby. We can try again when you're better. The seat belt tightened too quickly and damaged the placenta, but we're alive and have still got each other and Trudi. I'll always be here for you darling."

"What was it?" She felt she would never be happy again.

"It was a boy, but we've got plenty of time to try for another."

Larry's voice seemed to come from a long way off. His face was receding miles away into the ceiling. The bleeping steadied as she closed her eyes and stopped struggling.

"How's she doing?"

"She's coming round."

Ginny felt her fingers being squeezed. Tears overflowed from under her eyelids and ran down her cheeks.

"You have a good cry, my darling. You'll be fine. We'll be fine. Sandra at the NSPCC phoned last night; she's really got the ball rolling with Social Services and the Child Exploitation and Online Protection people. She said the home is going to be closed down, and the boys will be moved on. Now we've finally got the evidence the Vecks can be charged, along with all the other bastards involved. I'm going to hire Jared Colson-De'Ath to prosecute; he's the best in the business. We'll have to testify of course, but I'm with you all the way on this."

In her dazed state she could not comprehend what was happening. She felt her abdomen; it was flat and slightly hollowed. She wailed for her son, lying alone and half-formed in a kidney dish somewhere out of sight; just one of a long line of similar-looking kidney dishes on their way to the incinerator. *The baby that she and Larry had made with so much love was now dead, and nothing in the world could bring it back.*

At that precise moment she wished that whoever had slammed into the side of their car could have finished her off altogether.

"Where's Zac?" She whispered.

"Who?" Larry leaned in closer.

"The boy in the photo who was tied to the chair. We need to find him before they close the home."

"Why?"

"We have to adopt him." She coughed and opened her eyes. "Something good has to come out of all this; I want to give Zac a good life."

"We'll talk about it when you come home. Right now you need to get better so that we can go and get Trudi back."

"Promise me you won't forget Zac."

"I promise; I won't forget him."

For a month at least after the accident she would either sit staring into space or walk around the house in a dream, waiting for the baby to move inside her. She got into the habit of repeatedly looking down at her abdomen, feeling its soft lines and curves. The hardness of pregnancy had receded, and she found it difficult to come to terms with the sudden loss of all their exciting plans for the future.

She was aware that Larry was being as patient as he could be, but one day as she lay on the settee gazing at the ceiling, she saw him standing over her.

"Ginny, you've got to snap out of this. I need you; Trudi needs you. The baby's gone; I can't go on seeing you so depressed like this." Larry knelt down and took her hand in his. "I'm going to call the doctor in. You need some anti-depressants or something."

"No doctors. I'll come round in my own time." Ginny shook her head.

"The trial is coming up soon. Are you going to be well enough to testify?"

"If it's my last day on earth I'll be there." Ginny sat up and looked her husband straight in the eyes.

"Get well for me, baby." Larry kissed her tenderly.

"Can you do one thing for me?" She put her arms around him. "Remember your promise? This house needs more children. I need to find Zac."

"If it'll make you feel better I'll find Social Services' number now."

"You've got to want to do it, Larry; not just for me, you've got to want Zac as much as I do."

"I'll be back with the number sooner than you can say Jack Robinson, or maybe even Zac Robinson." Larry smiled at her.

"Thank you darling; thank you so much." Ginny sighed.

CHAPTER 29

THE ARLBOROUGH COURTS of Justice sat like a carbuncle on the back of the police headquarters. Ginny, holding Larry's hand, filed back in after lunch through the heavy oak doors of Court number one, and took her seat on the public bench. She was aware of Randolph Veck gazing inscrutably over in her direction, but kept her eyes on Judge Tomlinson as the court was brought to order. The judge put on her spectacles and sifted through her notes before addressing the jury.

"Mr Colson-De'Ath and Mr Fitzherbert have completed their summing up. I shall now ask the jury foreman to stand."

A middle-aged man clad in a dark blue pin stripe suit stood up nervously.

"Have the jury reached unanimous verdicts regarding the defendants?" The judge looked hopefully towards the foreman.

"We have, m'lady."

"Do you find Randolph Leslie Veck guilty or not guilty of the crime of indecent assault under section one of the Children and Young Persons Act of nineteen thirty three?"

"Guilty, m'lady." The foreman looked towards the dock.

"Do you find Dennis Alfred Veck guilty or not guilty of the crime of indecent assault under section one of the Children and Young Persons Act of nineteen thirty three?"

"Guilty, m'lady."

With a sudden release of tension, Ginny felt elated and somewhat light-headed. She was aware that Larry had risen to his feet amongst the ensuing hubbub of raised voices that could be heard all around the courtroom.

"Let the bastards hang!"

"Order!" The judge brought her gavel down upon the block.

"Sit down!" Ginny hissed at Larry and tugged at his jacket.

The foreman shuffled from foot to foot as silence once more settled over the court. Judge Tomlinson returned her gaze to the jury.

"Do you find Evelina May Veck guilty or not guilty of the crime of indecent assault as Accessory After the Fact under section one of the Children and Young Persons Act of nineteen thirty three?"

"Guilty, m'lady."

Ginny watched without compassion as the old lady fainted in the dock and was carried out in the arms of a policeman. She saw the Veck brothers' heads turn to follow their sister, and was brave enough to catch Randolph's eye as he once again swivelled around to face the judge. The frosty glare she received she knew would stay in her mind for many months to come.

"You can bet the world and his wife will be filing assault claims against them now going back years. Just you wait and see." Larry nodded in her direction and folded his arms in satisfaction.

"Do you find Archibald Ernest Wittlingson QC guilty or not guilty of the crime of indecent assault under section one of the Children and Young Persons Act of nineteen thirty three?"

"Guilty m'lady."

"Do you find Michael Patrick Farnes guilty or not guilty of the crime of indecent assault under section one of the Children and Young Persons Act of nineteen thirty three?"

"Guilty, m'lady."

Larry silently punched the air. The foreman wiped his brow. Ginny felt like doing a little dance around the courtroom.

"They'll never own up to Phil Desborough's murder, but at least they're going down for something." Larry squeezed her hand. "Who knows? Perhaps one day some evidence of that will come to light."

"Lastly, do you find Chief Inspector of Police Peter Hugh Greensmith guilty or not guilty of the crime of indecent assault under section one of the Children and Young Persons Act of nineteen thirty three?"

"Guilty, m'lady."

"Thank you ladies and gentleman of the jury. Sentencing will be one week from today. Court dismissed." The judge brought down the gavel and Ginny, sitting next to Larry, raised her hands to him for a high five.

CHAPTER 30

"ARE YOU STILL certain that you want to be foster parents?" Amelie Davidge jotted down some notes. "As we discussed last week, Zac Miles is a very challenging child. He has been in several foster homes, but sadly the families were not able to cope with him."

Ginny swept one arm around the room.

"As you can see, we have much to give a child such as Zac. He shall have our undivided attention, one-to-one tutoring with our daughter in the schoolroom, and we will encourage whatever talents he may have. We are quite wealthy, and he would not want for anything."

"How would your daughter feel at being displaced?"

"She is eight years old. Children adapt. It'll be good for her to have an older brother." Ginny sought Larry's hand on the settee, and felt a reassuring squeeze. "If you like I can call her down and you can ask her yourself. She is with her tutor now."

"Yes, we will need to speak to her at some point, but for now these early pre-approval sessions are for the would-be foster parents. I have to make an eventual recommendation to the fostering panel based on the information you give me."

"What do you need to know? Perhaps we can move this thing on a bit." Larry shifted impatiently on the settee. "How long does the process take?"

"It could be six months or more. As I said, we have to make a thorough assessment. I take it that Zac would have his own room?"

"Of course; not only his own room, but he would also have his own bathroom."

"I see." More notes were jotted down. "What about visits to his natural parents and family, putting aside any thoughts and feelings you have about them?"

Ginny felt a small *frisson* of jealousy surge through her body.

"Of course we would not want to stop Zac from seeing his mother and father. Has he any sisters or brothers?"

"He has three older sisters who have all left care now, and three younger brothers. His sisters have not kept in touch, but fortunately he still manages to see his brothers now and again."

"Wow; why can't they all be at home then?" Ginny spared a thought for a mother possibly grieving over for the loss of seven children.

"All the fathers of the children are absent, and his mother is a chronic alcoholic; the children were taken away at birth. His mother has been in and out of rehab for years, but unfortunately is not in a position to look after any of them."

"Poor woman, although I think if I'd had seven children taken away from me *I* would be an alcoholic too!" Ginny smiled at the social worker.

"Why do you want to be foster parents?"

Ginny thought Amelie Davidge had probably never laughed in her entire life. She looked towards the younger woman's left hand; there was no wedding ring present.

"As you know we discovered Zac under the most unusual of circumstances. The poor child has had an abysmal start in life. I want to try and bring some innocent fun back into his world, and hopefully in time the years of abuse he's suffered might start to fade."

"I don't think Zac will ever forget what has happened to him. His behaviour is a natural consequence of his upbringing." Amelie re-crossed her legs and took a sip of water.

"The perpetrators of the crimes against him are in prison now. Ginny's testimony helped put them away." Larry sat forward on the settee. "I hope he knows we're rooting for him. We want him in our family. As you can see we have a lot to give Zac."

"A child like Zac will need a lot of your time, energy, and love. He has obviously been sexually abused for years, although we were unaware of this. It might be that he never really recovers. You must be ready to be taken to the limits of your patience and endurance. He is one of the most challenging of our children. It would probably be wise to attend a few of our training sessions."

"Sure." Ginny nodded and looked at Larry, who shrugged his shoulders.

"Do either of you have to go to work?"

"I own a nightclub which I oversee the running of. It's not a nine to five job if that's what you mean." Larry shook his head. "Ginny is a writer."

"Oh?" Amelie looked in Ginny's direction.

"I write when I have the time. My first priority is to my family."

"What do you write about?" Amelie's pen poised over her notebook.

"Fiction usually; books that women like to read."

"I will have to read one. Do you have an agent?"

"I'm self-published; I'm hoping that when I finish my latest novel it may interest a literary agency this time."

"Good luck Mrs Ford; I have heard agents are like gold dust."

"You could say that." Ginny smiled wryly.

"Mr Ford; do you smoke?"

"No, and neither does Ginny."

"Are either of you receiving medical treatment currently?"

"No; I did have some physiotherapy a few months' back for a whiplash injury, but that's fine now."

"And how many units of alcohol do you drink each week?"

"The odd glass of wine or a can of beer. Ginny doesn't drink at all."

"Why is that?" Amelie turned away from Larry.

"I haven't drunk anything since before I was pregnant earlier in the year." Ginny shook her head to emphasise her words.

"Do you have another child?" Amelie took a covert glance around the room.

"I lost the baby in a car accident."

"I see. Mrs Ford…..." Amelie shuffled the papers on her lap and appeared uncomfortable. ….. "I just have to make sure that you want Zac for himself, and not to replace a lost infant."

"Oh no! I wanted Zac as soon as I saw him. My heart went out to him." Ginny sighed. "I have to tell you that we are not doing anything to avert another pregnancy, but even if I do have another child Zac will not suffer because of it."

"Thank you for your time today. I will plan the next visit when your daughter is not in the school room. I will need to talk to her about the possible disruption of her usual family life until Zac settles in. I need to find out how positive she is about gaining an older foster brother, and how she would feel about sharing your attention."

"We've already spoken to her. She's okay with it, but of course you will need to find out for yourself." Larry shrugged his shoulders and stood up. "I'll get security to open the gate for you. Thanks for coming." He shook the social worker's hand.

"Until the next time." Amelie turned to Ginny. "A pleasure to meet with you both."

"Goodbye." As Ginny shook the limp, clammy hand, she wondered excitedly what the future was going to bring.

CHAPTER 31

AT FIRST ALL she could see was Amelie Davidge standing in the open front porch clutching a suitcase, but Ginny soon became aware of a small figure hiding behind the social worker, who seemed to be shivering slightly even though it was unusually mild outside for early April.

"Come in Amelie! And is that Zac I can see there? Hello Zac! Nice to see you again!" Ginny put on her brightest voice and craned her neck around Amelie's small frame.

"We're here at last! Zac's really excited about coming to stay! He's been really looking forward to it!" Amelie stepped to one side, and her smaller and younger shadow immediately followed suit.

"You're just in time for lunch, Zac. Let me take that suitcase Amelie, and you're welcome to stay for lunch too."

"I have another case to see this morning, but I'll come back at the end of the week to see how Zac's doing." Amelie took hold of Zac's hand and led him into the hallway. "Now don't be shy; you've met Ginny before. Say hello." She smiled at him and held on to his hand.

Ginny kept a fixed smile on her face during the ensuing silence.

"He's probably hungry. Come into the kitchen Zac. You've met Larry and Trudi before, remember? There'll be some pizza and pasta for you."

There was no response from the boy. Ginny held out her hand at the same time that Amelie disengaged hers. Like a bolt of lightning Ginny watched as Zac took off at high speed and ran up the grand staircase.

"Zac!" Ginny called up the stairs as Larry wandered out of the kitchen.

"Where's he gone?" Larry looked about him.

"I don't know; he's been here a couple of times before. Maybe he's gone to his room. Hopefully he remembers where it is."

"He'll be down soon. I have to be off now. Just have your lunch and give him some time to adjust." Amelie backed towards the front door, eager to be gone.

"Where's Zac?" Trudi stuffed another piece of pizza into her mouth as Ginny and Larry entered the kitchen.

"He's run off upstairs. Let's leave him be for a while; he's probably a little upset and confused." Ginny sat down at the table, her appetite suddenly disappearing.

"Can I have his pizza?" Trudi began to reach over the table.

"No; when we've finished I'll go and try to coax him downstairs." Ginny chewed half-heartedly on some pasta, concerned as to what the boy was up to.

"Shall I go?" Larry put down his knife and fork and wiped his mouth with a serviette.

"No; you might be a bit heavy-handed. I'm not hungry now; I'll see if I can bring him down." Ginny stood up and looked towards the door.

"Shout if you need anything." Larry gave a thumbs-up sign.

Bridget and her girls had finished for the day, and the upstairs landing was quiet. Ginny tiptoed along the corridor, looking in each room as she passed. When she reached the guest suite that she had allocated as Zac's bedroom, the door was closed. Turning the handle, she poked her head around the door.

"Zac?"

She kept her voice deliberately quiet and entered the room, but the boy was not immediately visible. Ginny walked towards the en-suite bathroom, which was empty. A sixth sense told her to open the door of the walk-in wardrobe, where she was shocked to find a huddled figure sitting on the floor in the furthest corner.

"Hey Zac! There's some pizza downstairs for you!" Hiding her surprise and keeping her voice overly-cheerful, Ginny held out her hand to the boy. "Hurry, before Trudi eats it all!"

She saw the boy flinch as she extended her hand. Quickly retracting her arm, she kept her distance and kneeled down to face him in the doorway.

"I hope you'll get to like it here, Zac. Nobody here will ever hurt you, I want you to know that. I'm going to leave you alone now and go downstairs, but I'll put some sandwiches here in your room and a drink for you, as I think the pizza may be a bit cold by now. Come down when you're ready."

The boy remained silent and kept his eyes downcast. Ginny stood up and went downstairs, leaving the door to the guest room ajar. She returned with two rounds of sandwiches and left them on the bedside table.

CHAPTER 32

"YOU MUST HAVE been hungry, Zac! There's nothing left!"

No answer.

Ginny picked up the plate, empty bar a few crumbs, and stood helplessly by the bed.

"Can you swim? We have a heated pool outside. Do you have any swimming trunks in your suitcase? You're welcome to use the pool." She peered expectantly in the direction of the wardrobe.

"I can't swim."

Yes! Ginny sucked in a breath but kept her voice even:

"That doesn't matter at all. The pool has a shallow end, and Larry and I can teach you. If you feel like coming outside, we'll be having an evening swim soon. There's floats and things for you to play on."

No answer.

Ginny made to walk out of the room, plate in hand. As she reached the door she was aware of a small sound behind her. Turning around, she saw that Zac had ventured out of the wardrobe and was staring at her with eyes of the brightest blue.

"They never taught me in the home. They never bought me any swimming trunks." He returned his gaze downwards towards the floor.

"Okay, well that's easily solved. Tomorrow after school we'll go into town and buy you some. In the meantime why not come out and watch?"

"No."

"Fair enough. I'll leave you in peace then. You can see the pool though if you look out of your window. It'll be great if you can join us, but I understand if you want to be left on your own to settle in."

No answer.

"By the way, you'll be joining Trudi in the schoolroom tomorrow. Miss Argent is a lovely teacher." Ginny thought it best to remind the boy he was not there on a permanent holiday.

"I'm not going to school."

"You don't have to. Miss Argent comes here."

"Can't read. Don't want to go to school." Zac shook his head.

"All children have to go to school, but we'll talk about that in the morning."

"I'm not going!" Zac kicked a nearby chair leg, tipping the chair over. "You can't make me!" He stood defiant, hands on hips.

Ginny sighed, but felt relieved that at least she had managed to coax him out of the wardrobe.

"Zac; I would be fined heavily if you did not go to school. It doesn't matter that you can't read. Miss Argent will teach you."

"No!!"

The boy began to kick any furniture within reach. Ginny stepped back as she heard Larry running up the stairs.

"What's going on in here?" He looked around as he took quick stock of the situation.

"Zac says he's not going to school."

"Zac, please stop kicking the furniture!" Larry went towards the boy.

"Don't you touch me! Don't touch me!" Zac, arms and legs waving wildly, kicked and screamed at anything in sight.

Watching Zac's mild demeanour as it changed quick as lightning into a full-scale tantrum, Ginny looked worriedly at Larry.

"Good job we did the restraint training; you get one end and I'll get the other."

Larry shrugged his shoulders as he moved in closer and grabbed a firm hold of the boy. Within minutes he was a writhing bundle of fury on the floor. Ginny's heart went out to Zac squirming about helplessly; impotent and unable to move under their grip.

"You have to go to school, Zac. There's no choice. Make the most of there only being two of you in the class!" Ginny found it was taking all of her strength to hold him down.

"You fucking bastards! I hate you!" Zac's skinny body heaved with the strain of trying to escape.

"No you don't, Zac. You don't know us. We don't hate you. Come on, give us a chance!" Larry's voice was soft, but his grip was firm.

"Fuck off!"

"We don't use that language to each other, Zac." Larry's biceps bulged with the strain of keeping the boy still.

Ginny wanted to cry as the boy raged against her. Finally after what seemed like an eternity, his fury was spent, and he gave up struggling and burst into tears. Ginny released her grip and motioned for Larry to do the same. She stroked his hair as he lay unmoving, and smiled at Trudi standing in the doorway.

"We'll get to know each other, Zac. I hope you'll like it here. We're not bad people; we only want what's best for you. Miss Argent will teach you to read, and Trudi has lots of books that you can borrow. When we buy you some trunks tomorrow we can have a look around the shops and see if there's a book we can buy you that you like the look of."

Freed from their grip, Zac continued to lay still. Still stroking his hair, Ginny motioned with her other hand for Trudi to enter the room.

"Shall I go and find a book for you to look at, Zac?" Trudi edged in warily and stood behind her father.

Zac sobbed, but nodded at the same time. Trudi ran to her room as Zac slowly sat up:

"Shall I take my pants down now?" He began to unzip the front of his trousers.

Hiding her shock as best she could, Ginny shook her head and moved away.

"No, Zac. Your private place stays private. Please do your trousers up. Whatever has happened to you in the past, you have to know that it won't happen to you here."

As Zac zipped up his fly and looked confused, Ginny glanced at Larry and heaved a sigh of relief.

CHAPTER 33

"MRS FORD, MAY I have a word with you please?"

"Of course." Ginny smiled at Pat Argent and motioned for Marva to supervise the children's lunch. She followed the governess out of the kitchen, and directed her towards the sitting room.

"It's about Zac, Mrs Ford." Pat Argent appeared ill-at-ease.

"How's he doing?" Ginny's heart sank down to her boots.

"He's ten years old and he can't read a word." The tutor shook her head to emphasise the fact.

"I was afraid of that. How's his behaviour? Don't forget to ring the bell if he starts having a tantrum. All the security guys have been trained in restraint techniques. While Larry's out at the club I can call on one of them to help me. Steve's here today, so just let us know."

"No, no; he's quite withdrawn. I can't get two words out of him."

"He'll come round. He's only been here a few days. We have to give him time. Trudi's still got all her early reading books; shall I give them to you?"

"I'm still going through the alphabet and phonics at the moment. He's got a good memory though. He seems to have learned a few letters already."

"I'm sure he'll do very well eventually. I've promised him a dip in the pool after school today as a treat for behaving himself."

The governess seemed unwilling to leave. Ginny looked at her.

"Is there anything else?"

"Well, er………there is something."

"What?"

"Zac seems er……rather aware for his age."

"Aware? Aware of what?" With another sinking feeling Ginny tried to put off the inevitable, but realised exactly what the governess was talking about.

"Sexually aware, Mrs Ford. There's something not quite right about the child." Pat Argent blushed to the roots of her greying hair.

"What has he done?"

"Nothing I could see, but er….I think he knows more than most children his age."

"I'm afraid he's been sexually abused in the past. We're trying to teach him the correct way to behave, but it's not something that'll happen overnight. We need your help to reinforce good behaviour." Ginny felt awkward at the spinster's embarrassment. "If he does do anything that makes you feel uncomfortable, please let me know."

"Of course. Please excuse me. It's time for me to return to the classroom."

Ginny walked back to the kitchen, wondering if the governess was making mountains out of molehills.

"Miss Argent is waiting for you two upstairs. Have you finished your lunch?"

"Zac has." Trudi looked to her right. "I haven't."

"Okay Zac, if you go on back upstairs, Trudi will be up in a moment."

"Can I have some more, Ginny?" Zac's blue eyes shot right through her heart.

"What's the magic word?"

"Please." He looked hopefully towards the fridge.

"Okay; take some fruit up with you, and after school you can have a dip in the chocolate box before swimming."

With Zac on his way upstairs, Trudi watched her daughter happily stuffing her face.

"Has Zac been good this morning?" She kept her voice light and cheerful.

"Yeah, apart from showing me his willie under the desk." Trudi made a face.

"What did you say to him?" Ginny hid her shock as best she could.

"I had a look and then I told him to put it away." Trudi shrugged her shoulders.

"What did Miss Argent say?"

"She was writing on the blackboard, but she turned round as he did his trousers up."

"Don't worry; Mummy and Daddy will have a word with him."

Ginny knocked on guest bedroom door after Pat Argent had left, and gingerly opened it. On hearing the toilet flushing in the en-suite, she waited with Larry in the doorway until Zac emerged.

"Hi Zac. Good afternoon at school?" She smiled at him.

"It was okay." He looked at them warily.

"We just wanted to have a quick word with you before swimming."

"What?"

She drew a deep breath and followed Larry into the bedroom.

"Something happened in the classroom today that Miss Argent was not happy with."

"What? I haven't done anything!" Zac's voice rose in anger.

"We just need to tell you again to keep your private place private. Your trousers should stay done up at all times during the day unless you have to go to the toilet. Do you understand?" Ginny thought it best to keep Trudi out of the conversation.

"I didn't do anything!" Zac shouted. "She's telling lies!"

"Well; somebody is not speaking the truth, but whoever it is, the object of this conversation is to make sure you know how you're supposed to behave. Now we don't want Miss Argent to have to tell us again that she's not happy with the way you're conducting yourself." Ginny allowed a small smile to appear on her face. "However, we hear you're doing very well learning your letters."

"Keep on doing well with your reading, Zac, and we'll forget the other business this time." Larry ruffled the top of the boy's hair. "We'll leave you to get changed and then if you come out to the pool you can have a swimming lesson."

"Sorry Ginny; sorry Larry." Zac sighed and shifted from foot to foot.

"We're on your side, Zac. You just need to know the house rules." Larry smiled. "See you by the pool."

CHAPTER 34

"DO YOU THINK we've bitten off more than we can chew with him?" Larry opened the chest of drawers to search for his swimming trunks.

"I won't give up on Zac. Amelie's coming back tomorrow. We can discuss things with her."

"You're not swimming?"

"My period started this morning." Ginny hid her disappointment. "I wonder if I'll ever get pregnant again?"

"Perhaps it's best you don't at the moment. We've got enough to be getting on with. Have you done any writing lately?" Larry took off his sweatshirt and t-shirt and threw them onto the bed.

"No; I'm busy keeping an eye on Zac. I can't concentrate on anything else at the moment. Still; I'm glad we've got him though." She picked up the sweatshirt, still warm from her husband's body, and folded it neatly.

"What about Trude? D'you think it's too much to expect her to understand why we took him on?" Larry undid his trousers and took off his pants.

"Perhaps at the moment, but I think she's getting to like having him around." Ginny admired Larry's naked body. "Hmmm; my muscle man!" She smiled at him.

"Steady on; control yourself woman!" He laughed as he tied the drawstring on his trunks. "Where's a towel?"

"There's some out in the pool changing area for later."

"It's brass monkeys weather when you get out. Give us that sweatshirt back." He held out his hand.

"Come and get it!" Ginny raised her arm and twirled the sweatshirt around.

"Just as long as you don't grab my nuts."

"As if!" She laughed and kissed him as reached up and took the top from her hand.

"Love you Mrs Ford." He put his arms around her.

"Love you too. You'd best get out to that pool. The kids'll be there in a minute."

"I'd rather have sex with you." He nuzzled into her neck.

"I've got a period."

"I'll go then." He laughed and pulled the sweatshirt over his head.

Ginny walked along the landing and put her head around Trudi's bedroom door.

"Daddy's ready for swimming. How about you?" Searching the room, she was surprised to see Trudi sitting with Zac at her table, with their heads bowed over a book.

"I've got my cozzie on under my dress. I'm just helping Zac to read the page that Miss Argent wanted him to look at."

"Okay. When you've finished, come on out."

Larry was executing his usual perfect front crawl when Ginny, clad in a warm jacket, took a seat by the pool.

"Where's the kids?" Larry shouted out to her from under his arm as he carried on swimming.

"Trudi's helping Zac to read They'll be out in a minute."

"Great!"

She watched them as laughing, they ran down the steps to the pool area.

"Zac worked out a couple of words!" Trudi flung off her dress and jumped into the pool. "Come on in, Zac! It's warm!" She splashed some water in his direction.

Ginny picked up the day's newspaper but failed to read any of it as she kept half an eye on Zac, climbing gingerly down the steps into the shallow end of the pool.

"Hold on to this float if you like!"

Ignoring Zac's distress, Trudi swam like a fish over to where Zac stood shivering and holding on to the side rail for dear life.

"Come on; it's easy!" She threw the float towards him and dived under the water.

"Let him take his time; he's never been in the water before." Larry trod water nearby, "Zac, would you like me to help you?"

Terrified, Zac could only nod. Placing the boy's hands on the float and putting one arm securely around his waist, Larry shouted encouragement.

"That's it Zac! Kick with your legs; I've got you – you won't sink!"

Ginny put down the newspaper and clapped as Zac, with Larry's help, completed one width of the pool.

"That's terrific! We'll soon have you swimming in no time!" At that precise moment she felt genuinely sure that they had made the right decision in trying to integrate him into their family.

After an hour and with a smile as wide as the Cheddar gorge, Zac grudgingly climbed back up the steps to be enveloped by Ginny in a warm towel. However, as soon as the towel was wrapped around his body Ginny felt him shiver with something other than the cold. Immediately stepping back to give him his own space, she was aware that a sudden stream of yellow urine had left his body and was splashing onto the tiles as his gaze fixed upon the front page of the newspaper.

"What is it Zac? What's wrong?" She followed his gaze.

"That man!" Zac's eyes filled with tears as he pointed to a photo.

"Which man? What do you mean?" Ginny glanced at the newspaper and was surprised to see an article pertaining to Charles Standen of PhizzFace Inc.

"Him!" Zac dropped the towel and ran.

"What's up with Zac?" Larry hauled himself out of the pool and with both arms pulled Trudi out squealing.

"He looked at this photo of PhizzFace's new manager and was scared stiff. I recognise the name from when I worked there, but I never saw the guy." Ginny whispered and pointed to the ground. "He wet himself when he saw it."

"I don't recall seeing him before in the photos. Tell you what; I'll hose the tiles down and see to Trudi if you go and

find out what's wrong. He seems to respond more to you."
Larry shrugged his shoulders and threw a towel around Trudi.

The guest room door was closed. Ginny knocked softly.

"Zac. Can I come in please?"

No answer.

Turning the handle she peeped around the door but the room was empty. Making straight for the walk-in wardrobe she inched the door open to see Zac still wearing his damp swimming trunks, sitting morosely in one corner covered in goosebumps.

"Hey Zac. What's happened? Did you enjoy your swim?" Ginny knelt down on the same level as Zac, who nodded in reply.

"There's no need to be frightened here. Tell me what's wrong and I can do something about it."

As the boy shook his head, Ginny stood up and brought a towel back from the en-suite to place around the boy's shoulders. Zac pulled the towel to him and continued to look down at the carpet.

"Did the man in the newspaper do something to you?"

Ginny searched Zac's face for clues, but the boy's face was expressionless.

"Don't worry. Amelie's coming to visit tomorrow. I'll show her the newspaper and she'll be able to investigate."

CHAPTER 35

"MRS FORD! HOW are you?"

Ginny shook Amelie's hand, conscious of a small shadow behind her.

"Hey Zac; say hello to Amelie" Ginny looked behind her.

"Hello Zac!" Amelie peeped around Ginny's frame and smiled. "How have you been?"

"Okay."

Ginny was overjoyed to feel a small warm hand slipping in hers as they walked through the entrance hall to the sitting room.

"Hi Zac!" Steve waved from the security desk.

"He's called Steve." Zac, keeping his hand in Ginny's, addressed Amelie.

"I see you're making friends already." Amelie smiled at Steve.

"Steve lets me open and close the gate."

"I tell you what, Zac; if you run and play with Trudi for a while and let me speak to Ginny, I'll call you back down soon. Is that okay?"

"Trudi's with Larry out in the grounds by the swings. Do you remember where that is?"

As the boy nodded and ran off, Ginny motioned for the social worker to be seated.

"Can I get you some coffee or tea?"

"No, I'm fine thanks. I just want to say well done; you seem to be making some progress with Zac."

"We've had a few tantrums, but he knows we mean what we say. We try to be firm but fair."

"It's the only way to be." Amelie nodded. "How have you coped with his temper?"

"We've had to use the restraining techniques a couple of times, but again, we try and treat him the same as our own daughter. She knows that screaming won't get her what she wants, and I hope in time so will he."

"You've done marvels with him. The previous foster parents could hardly get him out of the wardrobe."

"He still goes in ours, but I wheedle him out usually. We're getting there slowly." Ginny chuckled and raised the palms of her hands. "Who knows if I'm getting through to him? Actually though he's now started following me around like a little duckling, and holding my hand."

"Ah; he likes you! He doesn't usually do that."

Ginny warmed to the social worker. She picked up the newspaper that she had previously placed on the settee.

"Zac saw this photo and flipped. I think he's another one of the PhizzFace paedophiles, although I don't recall ever seeing him when I worked there and he wasn't in any of the photographic evidence." She pointed to a smiling Charles Standen on the front page.

Amelie Davidge took the newspaper, reading the article with a nod of her head.

"Thanks for the info. We'll certainly look into this and see if we can come up with anything."

"That's great." Ginny smiled. "I'm sure there must be some evidence to convict him. And Amelie, I was thinking - would it be a good thing to invite some of the boys from the home here for tea, or something like that? I don't want Zac to miss out on seeing his friends."

Amelie shook her head.

"We'll do our best to keep him in touch with his family, but it's best he makes new friends. Perhaps take the children out of the grounds to the park where they can play with others? It might even be a good idea to enrol them in the local school."

Ginny nodded.

"Yes; we must think about that. We were too frightened for our own safety to leave, but now the ringleaders are no longer around it's time to try and integrate a bit more. I was actually thinking of getting in touch with the head teacher at Arlborough's private school. I think it's a good teacher to pupil ratio there." Ginny sighed. "I'm sure Sandra at the NSPCC told you everything that's happened to us. It's why we're fostering Zac in particular. We want to eventually adopt him and give him a good life."

Amelie folded up the newspaper and smiled.

"I'm sure Zac's going to have no concerns about being adopted by yourselves."

"That's great, but what about his birth mother?" Ginny voiced the problem that was concerning her most.

"She will obviously want some contact, but she knows she's in no state to look after him or any of the others. She's already agreed for three of her younger children to be adopted, and so we foresee no great problems in that department."

"Naturally we wouldn't keep Zac from his birth mother; we can arrange contact any time she wants." Ginny shrugged her shoulders.

"Other foster parents have had trouble with his behaviour when he's been to see her. He tends to be a bit unmanageable for a few days afterwards." Amelie put the newspaper into her briefcase. "She's asking to see him, but anyway, let's call him back in and see what he has to say."

Ginny picked up her mobile phone and scrolled down the contact list before dialling.

"Larry; can you send Zac back to the sitting room please?" She sipped from a glass of water while she waited. The grandfather clock ticked loudly as she desperately tried to think of another topic of conversation.

Thankfully, within a few moments the door to the sitting room opened and Ginny smiled as Zac came to sit close by her on the settee.

"Hello Zac!" Amelie's voice was brightly cheerful.

"Hi." Zac moved a little closer to Ginny.

"How are you getting on?"

"Okay."

"Do you like it here?" Amelie craned her neck forward to catch Zac's eye.

"Yeah."

"How do you like your new teacher?"

"She's alright." Zac kicked his feet against the bottom of the sofa.

"Miss Argent tells me you're learning your letters well." Ginny smiled and was rewarded with a grin from Zac.

"Yeah. I know them all now."

Amelie Davidge jotted down a few more notes.

"Zac; Ginny and Larry are very pleased that you're staying with them. Are you happy staying here longer?"

"Yeah." Zac's heels thrummed against the cream leather.

"Mum's phoned me; she would like to see you."

"Don't want to see her! I want to stay here!" Zac grabbed hold of Ginny's hand.

"It's only for the day, Zac. You'd come back here afterwards." Ginny squeezed the little hand and her heart went out to him.

"Mum's home from hospital now. Ginny and Larry can drive you there and pick you up at the end of the day." Amelie's smile was as bright as a summer's day.

"It smells in her house."

"She's well at the moment. I'm sure Mum'll clean up before you get there." Amelie studied Zac's face closely.

"She talks a load of rubbish; then she says the same thing again that she's just said." Zac sighed and shook his head.

"Mum can't help it when she's drinking; you know that, but as I said she's fine at the moment."

"If I have to." Zac sighed again. "Will Ethan, Michael and Aiden be there?"

Ginny's brain sprung into overdrive at the sound of Zac's final comment, and she turned to face him.

"Zac; who are Ethan, Michael and Aiden?" Her heart started to beat a faster rhythm in her chest as the names rang a bell in her brain.

"They're my little brothers; why?" He turned to look at her questioningly.

"Nothing; I just wondered. Have you got any more brothers?"

"No; I've got three older sisters though, but I don't know where they are." He shrugged his shoulders and turned towards the social worker again, who glanced at Ginny before popping the lid back on her pen.

"I'll have a word with their new foster parents and see if we can arrange for at least one of them to come, but I think Mum might find four of you a bit too much to cope with." Amelie smiled and closed her notebook. "Well that's settled!" She stood up and picked up her briefcase. "I can see you're doing really well, Zac. I'll phone Ginny about which day you can see Mum, and then I'll come back and see you in a fortnight. You can go back and play with Trudi now."

As Zac ran off, Ginny raised her arm.

"Er…..Amelie. Can I have a quick word with you before you go?"

"Sure! What is it?" Amelie turned and rested her briefcase on the coffee table.

"Zac's brothers; I've just remembered where I've seen their names before."

"Oh?" Amelie looked up with interest.

"Their names were on the memory stick that I found at PhizzFace. I'm certain they've been abused by the Vecks too!" Ginny nodded and felt nauseous all over again.

"They've never said anything to us." Amelie looked stunned at the revelation.

"They're probably too terrified to say anything. Zac hasn't mentioned the Vecks yet, either. We're just hoping that one day he might trust us enough to talk about it." Ginny sighed and shook her head. "Those poor kids; Evelina probably wangled her way into the home, showered gifts on the kids like a bona fide benefactress, while all the time finding out which ones never had any family or visitors. She's just as evil as all the others."

Amelie held out her hand.

"Thanks so much for letting us know. We had no idea Zac and his brothers were being sexually abused. The staff at the home gave us no information We just thought Mum couldn't cope due to alcoholism."

"Evelina undoubtedly paid them off." Ginny shook the proffered hand.

"We'll make sure the boys get some counselling." Amelie walked towards the door.

"Thank you. I'll see you out."

Ginny signalled to Steve to open the gate, and then walked Amelie to her car.

CHAPTER 36

CHARLES STANDEN LOCKED his office door and walked along the corridor towards the lift. As he walked he scuffed his shoes into the PhizzFace logo on the carpet. *His mother had been correct as usual; she had always told him that everything would come to those who waited. And he had waited a long time. He missed her. She had been dead ten years now; she would never know. Such a shame.*

He had always hated those Friday evenings. It had never been about the kids as far as he was concerned; hell, he and Sue had produced five of their own and he had never touched a hair on any of their heads. No, it was about being second best. It was about being the bastard child of Aldous Veck and knowing he would never be able to take over at the helm. It was about thick Rupert Veck not even being able to find his dick in the dark but the company would probably still default to him in the end anyway. It was about his mother having to plead with Aldous to get him a job. It was about all the years he had to work his way up from the factory floor while Randolph and Dennis looked down on him from above. It was about his mother never having enough money or clout to lift the fucking gagging order. Well, he had amassed enough money now; fifteen years of working in Randolph's shadow and keeping a low profile had seen to that, plus a little 'manipulation' of the monthly figures.

Charles pressed the button to call the lift. While he waited he looked up and down the pristine corridor; *Bob Fenton's girls were doing a grand job.* He thought about the one called Ginny, the one who had found his memory stick, although now he could not recall her face at all. *He knew she would have found it eventually though, because Evelina had told him at the time that not only was she a good little cleaner, she was also a writer, and that would have made her intelligent. That other one, Emma, had never found it but somehow she had known something funny was going on. She had had to go.*

All the time he'd spent gathering secret photos for evidence, and his half-brothers had never suspected a thing; had not even the foggiest idea they had been caught on camera or had another brother. Randolph and the others had always been ruled by their loins, but he, Charles, had always had a good business head on his shoulders. His mother had always told him that someday he would be able to run the company; it was his birthright, and now with Randolph, Dennis and Evelina out of the way, and having to pay out millions in genuine (and bogus too — he would see to that) compensation claims, her prophecy had come to fruition. He would let John Ridley stay, even though he knew he had once been Randolph's closet boyfriend. John was a good guy, and good guys who kept their mouths shut were hard to find. Rupert was a pushover because he was idiotic and gullible; Charles could easily take care of him.

However, to make sure the Vecks were all out of the running for good, he would now have to drum up some sort of evidence to link them to the death of that nosey private investigator. Surely it could not be too difficult to point the police in the right direction? Evelina's security guy was another one who had always had shit for brains, and he'd had no idea they were being followed that night. It had been quite fortuitous that he, Charles, had spotted that chap sitting in his Volvo and had tipped thick Freddie off just in time. Freddie didn't know what day it was, but he was strong, and you knew that you would always want him on your side in a fight.

The lift doors opened. Charles stepped in, and pressed the button to descend to the underground garages. On exiting he looked with disdain upon his shiny black Mondeo.

Enough already! Time to buy a Ferrari!

PART THREE – FIVE YEARS LATER

CHAPTER 37

"AIDEN, YOU LITTLE shit! Get that mouse out of Mickey's sleeping bag!"

Ginny, sitting on the steps of the motorhome whilst Trudi slept on in ignorant bliss, savoured the misty morning air and stifled a giggle as she listened to the early morning male conversation emanating from the supersized tent pitched alongside.

"It wasn't me, it was Ethan!"

"Was not! It was Aiden!"

"I don't care who it was; get it out….now! Mickey, shut up whinging!"

Zac's deep *basso profundo* carried far across the field. Ginny glanced around guiltily, but no other campers seemed to be stirring. She watched as a small hand unzipped the outer part of the tent and ejected a small brown rodent by its tail, which scampered off thankfully into the long grass.

"If you lot don't shut up in a minute, we're going home!"

Ginny's shoulders shook with suppressed laughter as Larry emerged from the tent, yawning and scratching his head.

"What are you laughing at? It's alright for you two, kipping in luxury. I'm stuck in there with that lot!" Larry pointed at four grinning faces framed in the tent's opening.

"You love it really!" Ginny hugged her knees with mirth.

"Oh yeah; it's right up there with my hernia operation. Sling me a towel; I'm going for a shower."

Ginny stood up, padded to the small cupboard, and returned carrying a bag of toiletries and a towel which she threw in her husband's direction.

"These are yours I think." She turned towards the tent. "Zac; if you can top up the water please, then I'll get the coffee going."

"Okay."

With great ease, Zac slid from the tent and hoisted the capacious plastic water container into his arms, entered the motorhome, and poured its remnants into a saucepan.

"Thanks Zac. How does sausages and scrambled eggs grab you?"

"Sounds great. I know it was Aiden who found that mouse. He can have bran for breakfast; he'll be so busy running backwards and forwards to the toilet block that he won't have time to wind anybody else up."

Ginny laughed and watched fondly as Zac, six feet tall at the last measurement, jumped down the steps and rapidly caught up with Larry, who was already halfway to the showers. She then turned on the gas cooker, poured some oil into a frying pan, and set the saucepan of water to boil as thirteen year old Trudi threw back the duvet and fished around for her slippers.

"What was all that arguing about?"

"Aiden put a mouse in Mickey's sleeping bag."

"Ugh! He's so gross!"

"It's what little boys do. Aren't you glad you have four brothers?"

"No."

"They're not too bad, as boys go; Zac keeps them in order."

"He's alright; it's Aiden who's the pain." Trudi looked at herself in a small mirror and combed her hair. "I think I've got a wrinkle." She peered closer.

"Get to forty like me, and then you'll know what wrinkles are." Ginny sighed and turned the flame up under the saucepan.

"Get some of that cream from where you used to work then." Trudi brushed a stray strand of hair from her eyes.

"I'd rather have the wrinkles. There's no way I'd want to give any of my money to that company, *and* it's over one hundred pounds a jar now." Ginny smiled ruefully at her daughter.

"Can't I have a sister instead?" Trudi pouted in the mirror and applied some lipsalve. "Why don't you adopt a girl?"

"I'm too old for having babies, and we have enough children already. Be grateful for what you've got."

"I've got four morons for brothers."

"Well, at least you haven't got to worry about being bullied at school with Zac around."

"I suppose so."

Larry returned from the shower block and joined in a spontaneous game of football, still holding the toiletry bag and with a wet towel over his shoulder.

"Come on boys, breakfast is ready!" Ginny swirled the sizzling sausages around in the pan at the same time as ensuring the scrambled eggs remained uncharred.

"I'm vegetarian." Trudi sniffed.

"Since when?" Ginny looked at her daughter in surprise.

"Since today. It's cruel to kill pigs for my breakfast."

"I haven't killed any pigs today, darling." Ginny placed the hot sausages on some kitchen paper to drain.

"I'll have hers then!" Ethan leapt up the stairs to the motorhome and stood in the doorway. "Trudi can have bran!"

"You're all *uber* gross!" Trudi picked up a dry towel and a pile of clothes. "I'm going for a long shower!"

Shrugging her shoulders, Ginny shared out the mess of eggs, adding two sausages to each plate. Within a short while a plague of human masculine locusts had demolished every last scrap of food from the pans.

"No need to worry about leftover food here!" Ginny smiled as she watched the boys mopping up juices from the sausages with thick slices of bread.

"Us boys are washing up while Ginny goes for a shower."

Larry's authoritarian tones stopped the younger boys in their tracks as they tried to leave the table. Ginny grabbed the last dry towel and escaped across the field to the shower block.

CHAPTER 38

"IT'S NICE HERE. I've enjoyed the holiday." Zac, sweating and breathless, came and plonked himself down next to Ginny on the steps of the motorhome "I'm not in the game anymore; Trudi just caught me out."

"So I see; I'm hopeless at rounders. I was out as soon as I tried to bat." Ginny laughed and moved sideways to make more room.

"Aiden's the one to have on your side. He's like a little rocket." Zac pushed his hair out of his eyes and smiled.

"He's fast; no doubt about that." Ginny watched Aiden run like a whippet around all four posts. "No wonder he eats like a horse."

As he watched his brothers running and laughing, Ginny was aware that Zac had bowed his head. She heard a small sob escape from his lips:

"He was only six and Mickey was five. I couldn't help them. Ethan was eight; I was their big brother Ginny, and I couldn't help them."

As Zac wiped away a tear, Ginny put an arm around his shoulders.

"Zac, it's okay; you were only ten years old yourself. You were weak and powerless. You mustn't blame yourself."

"But I do! I should have protected them!" Zac caught his breath and sighed.

"You were too young. There was nothing you could have done to stop it." Ginny looked up and saw Larry glancing in their direction.

"If they ever get out of jail they'd better be looking over their shoulders."

As Zac's strong hands bunched into fists, Ginny gave him a squeeze.

"No, Zac; if you harmed them you would end up in prison, and they would have ruined your adult life as well as your childhood. Don't let them get to you; they're in prison now. Let them stay there; it's where they belong."

Ginny could see Zac's jaw tightening and relaxing with the stress of unburdening himself.

"That old woman used to bring us toys and sweets and pretend she was a friend of my mum's. We didn't know her, but we were too excited to be given presents and chocolate to wonder who the hell she was."

"Amelie told me she died last year. That's one of them out of the running anyway." Ginny shook her head as she saw Larry heading towards them.

"Good. I often wonder why the home didn't check up on her. She was an evil bitch." Zac ran a hand across his eyes and sighed again. "Thank God they got that other one as well. Mr Charles, we had to call him; but the worst one was

Mr Randolph. I hated that bastard so much. He always said that if any one of us spoke about what went on, we'd all have our tongues cut out."

"Let it go, Zac. We're here for you. It's so good that we've finally talked about it."

With a tortured sob, Zac put his hands to his face and cried. Ginny wrapped her arms around him and held him tightly, as across the other side of the field she saw Larry signalling and tactfully keeping the rest of the children amused.

"Mickey's dad used to come to the home a few times to see him. I used to sit on the windowsill and watch him walk up the drive. I wanted him to take us all away, but he never did. One day he just stopped coming. I'm never going to get married or have kids. I'm so fucked up I can't think straight!" Zac's sobs escalated as his whole body rocked in distress.

"That's where you're wrong, Zac. One day you'll find somebody to love and who loves you, and you'll be the best Dad in the world because of what you've been through. You'll know the best way to treat your children." Ginny cuddled him as her own eyes filled with unshed tears.

"Why couldn't you have been my mum?" Zac sniffed as Ginny passed him a tissue from her bag.

"I wish I could have been, but your mum's really trying to recover now. She looked so much better the last time we saw her."

"She should never have had us. She doesn't love us. I should never have been born."

"Your mum does love you; you mustn't forget that, but she's an alcoholic and possibly always will be. The drink has made a mess of her life, but it's not for anyone to say who can have babies and who can't. We just have to make the most of our lives when we're here. Larry and I are so happy we have you, and we love you all. I was only given Trudi, and that's how it is. I've tried to make the most of my life by adopting you and your brothers, and you've all brought such joy into our house. We want to give to you all that we never had as children, and by some strange quirk of fate we are able to do just that." Ginny gave Zac another squeeze. "Dry your eyes, Zac; you're young, with the rest of your life to enjoy. It's best to look forward and put the past behind you."

Zac dabbed at his eyes, and Ginny was relieved to see a thin smile play about his lips.

"Thanks for everything you've done for us. I'm so sorry."

"No problem, and there's nothing to be sorry about. All you've got to do now is to show your brothers and Trudi who's the best at fielding when it's their turn to bat!"

EPILOGUE

THE LAST CHAPTER of the novel was finally complete; all in all 'For the Sake of a Child' had taken her more than five years to write. With some satisfaction Sandra Mevo typed 'THE END' and stretched her arms over the back of her black leather chair. The muted sounds of excited children splashing about in the swimming pool outside could be faintly heard through the open office window, accompanied by the occasional shout from her husband Ali when things were getting out of hand.

Sandra smiled and turned off the computer. Two literary agents had expressed an interest in the first few chapters, and had now asked for the manuscript. She had a good feeling about this book; her previous teen romances had bombed, but at last this one was gaining some interest.

Okay, so she had had to change the perpetrators' details a little bit; drug addicted stepfathers abusing children in their charge was a little too common these days to interest the reading public. She had managed to do what was commonly known as 'sexing it up' to get the attention of the agents; a rich, powerful, good-looking man, an anti-ageing cream that everyone wanted, and an evil old lady seemed far more glamorous than the reality of four ignorant, drugged-up stepfathers on a council estate and an alcoholic mother.

She stood up and wandered over to the window. She could just make out some movement through the shrubbery surrounding the pool. She chuckled on hearing her daughter Tammy whining to her father that somebody had just splashed her while she was trying to read. Ali's response was too faint to make out, but Sandra could easily imagine what her husband was saying.

"Don't get a gob on – either splash him back or go inside!"

Dear Ali; always on a short fuse, but she loved the bones of him; such an excellent father to Tammy and to the four adopted boys. With Ali's inheritance they had bought this lovely house, and as soon as she saw it she knew it needed the sound of children's voices. After her ectopic pregnancy and emergency hysterectomy she had to accept that Tammy would be an only child, but there was no reason why they could not adopt. They had only been in their mid-thirties, and Social Services had welcomed them with open arms.

Leon, Steven, Philip, and Andrew. Poor little damaged darlings; one by one over the years, drug and alcohol problems had carried off all their parents. She hoped against hope that none of them inherited their parents' addictive natures, but only the passage of time would tell. She had managed to weave their real names into the story, but their true identities needed to be masked of course. Sixteen year old Leon, naturally taciturn, had already read the story and had grudgingly nodded his approval, but she would have to leave showing it to the younger ones until they were a few years older.

However, it would have been nice to have had all those staff members; security guys, cooks, nannies, and gardeners, but it was a lovely fantasy to write about. Ali's money would only stretch so far, but at least looking after the house and children gave them something to do and filled their days. There was always the nightclub of course to bring in extra money, but the days needed to be free for the children.

Sandra yawned and turned towards the door.

She needed some exercise, and a dip in the pool would be just the thing. She smiled a secret smile; one day she might even call Ali's bluff and actually go for a midnight swim in the nude. He was always going on about it. She could just imagine what the expression on his face might be like if she turned around and said yes - ha ha! One day she would do just that to surprise him, and you never knew what might happen beneath the water if there were only the two of them around..............

THE END

If you have enjoyed this book you may also like *A House Without Windows* by Stevie Turner.

REVIEWS OF 'A HOUSE WITHOUT WINDOWS'

"Devastating, creepy, and deeply affecting, Stevie Turner's A House Without Windows is many things: among them are several different, disturbing love stories. There is a tale of abduction, imprisonment and menace, a narrative of a woman clinging to hope in the face of utter despair, and a portrait of the claustrophobic world of a victimized child and the tormented adult she becomes . The multiple, shifting narrators effectively portray the disorienting madness of Edwin Evans and the effects of his psychotic actions on every victim his insanity engulfs.

Definitely not for kids, but highly recommended, indeed." – *Thom Stark*

"Written with true excellence, encompassing multiple perspectives, this novel is apt to leave the reader feeling absolutely drained as the suspense builds slowly and inexorably, achieving some incredible emotional climaxes along the way. It's a powerful work that comes across as realistic, making the reader feel what it might be like to be held captive and despairing over the thought that he or she might never be re-united with their loved ones. An absolute must-read for people who take their reading seriously!" - *Aldo Ray fan*

OTHER BOOKS BY STEVIE TURNER

A HOUSE WITHOUT WINDOWS
THE PILATES CLASS
FOR THE SAKE OF A CHILD
LILY: A SHORT STORY
NO SEX PLEASE, I'M MENOPAUSAL!
A RATHER UNUSUAL ROMANCE
THE DAUGHTER-IN-LAW SYNDROME
REVENGE
THE NOISE EFFECT: A SHORT STORY
THE DONOR
LIFE: 18 SHORT STORIES
MIND GAMES
REPENT AT LEISURE
A NOVELLA COLLECTION
LEG-LESS AND CHALAZA: A DARK NOVELETTE
A MARRIAGE OF CONVENIENCE